Duels

THE FRENCH LIST

RECENT TITLES IN **THE FRENCH LIST**

Hélène Cixous

Mdeilmm

Translated by Peggy Kamuf

Fabienne Kanor

Old World

Translated by Lynn E. Palermo

J. M. G. Le Clézio

On the Wrong Side

Translated by Joyce Zonana and Janet Lee

Shmuel T. Meyer

And the War Is Over . . .

Translated by Gila Walker

Makenzy Orcel

The Emperor

Translated by Nathan H. Dize

Cécile Wajsbrot

Nevermore

Translated by Tess Lewis

Néhémy Dahomey

Duels

Translated by
Nathan H. Dize

LONDON NEW YORK CALCUTTA

Seagull Books, 2025

First published in French as *Combats* by Néhémy Pierre-Dahomey

First published in English translation by Seagull Books, 2025

ISBN 978 1 8030 9 559 2

British Library Cataloguing-in-Publication Data
A catalogue record for this book is available from the British Library

Typeset by Seagull Books, Calcutta, India

To my father
who did everything he could

To Tiphaine Samoyault
for bringing my work to light

CONTENTS

1

After hearing that her husband had just acknowledged the bastard of a negro woman from the hills, Ludovic Possible's mother spent six weeks stewing in a pool of indignation until she drew her last breath, suffocated by anger. Ludovic was only twelve years old. Etched in his memory was the image of his dying mother praying her rosary between fits of vomit and plaintive whining. Doctors concluded it was a case of typhus or Gaol fever, but young Ludovic favoured another idea surrounding his mother's death. 'Mama died of shame,' he often told himself, 'Adultery was what killed her.' In death, his pale-coloured mother turned dark blue, the colour of disgrace. Over the years, Ludovic never failed to see in this the sentimental rather than the medical source of his mother's bad luck.

More than sixty years later, on the day of his wife's accidental death, Ludovic Possible was overwhelmed by the deadliest poison of all: shame. Hoping to steel himself against it, he decided to abandon his large house in the village of Croix-des-Bouquets, the administrative capital of the Cul-de-Sac plain, and settle on his farmlands.

Like most mulattos of his age, Ludovic fashioned himself a third leg out of oak—a superb cane with a silver handle featuring the piratical motif of a skull and two crisscrossed sabres. He was never seen wearing a frock coat. Come rain or thunder, he was always sporting flannel trousers, held up by the same grey suspenders over his linen shirt the colour of storm clouds. He carried his bones about, chained together by a pronounced network of veins, held fast by skin.

Ludovic traversed the village of Croix-des-Bouquets and presented himself at the offices of Éric Saurel, the district commandant, representative of the communes and guarantor of public authority.

*

According to the hierarchical organogram laid out on parchment and locked in the desk drawers of highly ranked individuals, the district commandant—the local point of contact for the commander-in-chief, the president of the Republic—is the one who ensures public safety, the civility of citizens and the proper functioning of institutions. The district commandant coordinates the actions of commune commandants and receives a copy of every written agreement, whenever there is one, every bilateral contract drawn up before a notary, diligently completed, dated and signed beneath the coat of arms of the Republic in the lower right-hand corner of the page. As for District Commandant Éric Saurel, he does not owe his high powers to the previous formal verbiage. His secret is something else altogether: Éric Saurel has been around since forever. A wily old soldier, Saurel is a veteran of the Indigenous Army of Haiti, lined up front and centre, as he loves to say, during the war for national independence. He hardly speaks but drinks heavily. He pleases the wealthy without ever really humiliating the poor city dwellers or peasants. Commandant Saurel presently enjoys all the benefits of every civil and military title, without ever defining any of them or limiting his own ambitions.

Ludovic Possible paid no attention to the young, unarmed soldier sitting cross-armed next to the door in the hall, his eyes staring straight ahead, engrossed in the silence of his chair. He walked into Éric Saurel's office, a large, well-lit room at the centre of the commandant's house, opposite his bedroom.

'Let's open a school in the town of Boën,' Ludovic hurled at Saurel without a greeting.

Éric Saurel stopped reading and lifted his head. He was not surprised by such an appearance. The visitor was round like a cat, his face covered in ashen sideburns and the words seemed to slip out on their own from between his thin lips.

'The rural code only forestalls a notary,' Commandant Saurel replied.

'I'll be the notary then,' Ludovic concluded.

He left just as he had arrived.

*

Once in Boën, a place he knew quite well, Ludovic grasped the extent to which the plains were cut off from the rest of the country, isolated from the world. Nobody knew who lived or died there. The inhabitants of Boën grew like plants, multiplied like their horses and rotted like overripe fruit. So good old Ludovic Possible, also known as Papa Possible, found himself in the role of notary—though his initial intention had been to establish a school. The administrative manager was tasked with incorporating the peasants of Boën into the national portrait.

Ludovic Possible now oversaw the registry in the plain: agrarian conflicts, debt contracts between the peasants or marital agreements that grandmothers in their thirties negotiated on the behalf of descendants not yet emerged from the womb. He also recorded, as best he could, the dates of births and deaths, possessions in heads of cattle and all the first names in groups of siblings. Sometimes suitors came to see him with their beloved ladies for him to record the promises of eternal love in exchange for sexual consent.

Papa Possible became the open book of the Cul-de-Sac plain. There was no longer any need to travel all the way to Croix-des-Bouquets, for as soon as the people from Boën got into the habit of coming to him, locals from elsewhere appeared, and for the time being, he was open to receiving people from all around. Those from Mardelle, oh so belles! And from Peyrac? They came as a pack! All the way from O'Gorman, each and every one! One came from Juan, fainting from too much sun! And like an anthill came the people of Vaudreuil! So many picturesque places with slogans behind their names, ready to shine bright during the country games. Only the farmers who worked their own land never came to visit Possible the notary. Their absence was not due to any obvious conflict of interest but because, as they say, a man who knows how much you earn has no right to know of whom or of what you dream.

*

It was a fact that many farmers came to trust Ludovic Possible, widening his notarial reach, much as they would in a confessional booth or simply to share their dreams with him. At first, he tried to interrupt them, reminding them that a notary did not note everything. But he eventually capitulated, and by now his visitors have no idea what his title means: they come, they testify and they leave. Along with their dreams, Ludovic Possible learnt that farmers eat meat every night, that the devil wears Napoleon's little hat, that the Supreme God, Bondye, is a little girl, that men delight in their sisters-in-law, that women often strangle their husbands and that paradise has no soldiers. Not to mention their shared nightmare: to leave this place, to walk and walk only to find themselves in the same life, standing in front of the exact same house.

Yet Master Possible did not abandon his goals as an educator. Over the months and years, he instructed the children of the plain without codes or constraints. He certainly knew how to read and write, but he was never destined for the teaching profession; besides, no man is a school unto himself, so to speak —there needed to be walls, personnel or the even slightest bit of furnishings. In the end, the children built what could be called an educational establishment on their own, beginning with the building, the curriculum and a grading system. It was quite simple: every day after the morning dew, Ludovic welcomed children of all ages, depending on the season and everyone's availability, starting with his own great-grandchildren, Jean-Zamor and Doréus, a few of his nieces and nephews and the mysterious little girl named Aïda, whom he sought out himself.

Truth be told, Papa Possible's initiative bore all the marks of his bullheadedness. It would have bordered on ridiculous had he not been a well-respected landowner and the only notary in the area. His backyard was large enough to accommodate a pack of seventy well-fed pigs, not to mention the countless chickens that could lead a peaceful life around the house. He liked asking the farmers to send their children because, as he believed, education was sacred—the future of the world. He even went so far as to raise the credit rate for those who brought in most children. In response to this conspicuous generosity, some adolescents came to help their parents, sparing themselves from the arduous herding of animals.

As for the girl, Aïda, she loved being around these boys, running around and learning together what none of them knew particularly well. At twelve and eight months, she wore her body like a bulky sack and let her head flutter about in unknown worlds. Ludovic Possible did not really give her mother a choice. Aïda found herself there, staring silently and sometimes imitating the others. When it came to building things—a bench, a table or even a new schoolhouse—she contributed what she could with her scrawny arms. She would not accept being pushed aside for any reason. Even without speaking, her stubbornness was hard to break. She stayed glued to the older children, never asking for anything, but refusing to budge unless she too had a piece of wood to carry or some thatch to weave. When other children, out of sheer malice or boredom, decided to give her a dust bath or to pull her hair, she unleashed one of her horrible shrieks that cut through the braying of donkeys and the crowing of cocks. She shot them a defiant glance and then picked up her silence where she had left it, almost participating like the others, or at least most of them. This sonorous defence kept the others at bay, isolating Aïda enough to create around her an aura of mystery and fear.

From the day he defended her against an older girl, only Jean-Zamor, Ludovic Possible's great-grandson, had managed to break through her aura. Jean-Zamor was already thirteen years old. With his sweat and his fists, he defended Aïda against the pervasive persecution, against the other whiny children who accused her of being nothing more than a shameful girl, a sorceress. They said she was born wicked, that she had an evil spirit or that she was born with a full head of hair. Jean-Zamor too acknowledged his friend's magical powers, but for a good reason! Last November, he came upon her when she was in the middle of a conversation with one of the coconut trees on the main road, not far from Papa Possible's house.

In her blue camisole dress, fluttering in the wind, Aïda asked the tree to throw the Chief Corporal from its crown, completing a final act of collective hostility.

*

The time had come to attempt another census. Since Ludovic Possible had arrived in Boën, Commandant Éric Saurel—his superior under the present circumstances—saw an opportunity to impose a certain *militarized agriculture* on the countryside. This meant the strict application of the rural code of 1826: control the peasantry and turn it into a forced reserve for the new, heavily indebted Military State. None of these projects could proceed without a detailed survey of the countryside, its inhabitants, their children and their property. For this reason, Commandant Saurel delegated his nephew, the young agent Pierre Saurel, to oversee the census.

Embarking on his journey—solitary as Christ himself—the wholly affable, thirty-year-old Corporal Pierre Saurel expected a little resistance. But he could never have anticipated such hostility. None of the peasants or the notables granted him the slightest hospitality promised in his dispatch papers. He was forced to spend many cold nights in an old hammock, with the sky for a roof and his clothing for cover, suspended between two coconut trees declared free for public usage. Joined by two officers with the inflated title of 'aide de camp', or field aid agents, they erected a tent, which only deepened the contempt of the local Boënnais, who spoke of them as new colonists. Everyone, right down to the dogs, barked at their arrival. Ludovic Possible, who could easily have lent a helping hand by sharing his notes with Pierre Saurel in keeping with his position as titular notary, was the first to oppose the census. Ludovic never even spoken to Saurel, from the time of his arrival to the moment when the Corporal fell fifteen metres from a coconut tree shouting, 'Save yourselves!' as though it were the most expressive of all curses.

The unfortunate Corporal fell out of the coconut tree just after Aïda's request, echoing the public protest. He lay at the base of the tree as if in the middle of a nap, without a drop of blood, his mouth agape, a rivulet of blue drool dripping from his tongue.

2

More than three months after that sudden death, the men and women of Boën had not yet been counted, and the backyard school—the perfect polling station for such an occasion—kept grinding along.

Inside, you would find a few inkwells and quills, slates for the limestone chalk the students had themselves made, scrolls of parchment paper, a dozen syllabaries and three books of mathematics. One of them—not an arithmetic book—was so unfamiliar that everyone agreed that it must have been written in a language unknown to humans. There is also a storage shed full of curious objects, including two large chests left behind by some parents in lieu of the time they could not afford to contribute to the school—parents who never came to help care for the students. These were the same parents whom no one asked to share their life stories, as though they might qualify as historical material. Yet the truth was this: the country was so new that everyone was, in their own way, a historical figure. Telling one's life story was as much an act of storytelling as it was of setting an example for tomorrow, while talking about other countries revealed as much about political geography as it did the comparison of eras. Just a few nautical leagues from here, for example, in the vast territory of the twenty-six states of North America, the barbarity of slavery continued as in the centuries past, lost beneath the filthy claws of history, and the courageous word 'negro' still belonged to the macabre register of insult. Many an extraordinary lesson was learnt under the tutelage of Ludovic Possible, who—without expecting or asking for it—reaped rewards of guinea fowl, sacks of provisions, tobacco leaves and cacao plants.

The parents also contributed coverless books, unearthed from who knows where, which they shoved into the chests in the storage shed. They did this so often that Ludovic finally had to place a sign beside the chests that read: 'The school no longer accepts book donations. Thank you for your understanding.' Since most of the parents could barely read the words 'thank you', the book donations multiplied. In the end, the door to the shed was blocked off, and Ludovic threatened to unleash the dogs on whomever trespassed onto his property—even with a single book.

*

Apart from the school, Ludovic Possible kept three dogs in his backyard: a spaniel and two greyhounds. The well-acknowledged vivacity of these beasts did not spell good news for chicken thieves. Worse still, should it bear repeating, Papa Possible never owned a single chicken. As for the dogs, they were now called Ti Beau, Le Maître and Le Grand, names chosen by Aïda, although they had once been called The Frenchman and The Cubans, in reference to the hounds the cruel General Rochambeau of the French Army brought from Cuba to aid his colonial troops during the war for independence. If it is said that Rochambeau introduced only Newfoundlanders into battle, it is equally true that the spaniel, Ti Beau, came from Paris, while the two greyhounds were identical to those used on Cuban plantations to hunt down maroons.

When Ludovic settled down in Boën five years ago, he brought his dogs with him, hoping to re-establish what remained of his family. Soon enough, however, these pups proved a nuisance in his new life as a retiree, and for a time he considered sending them back to Croix-des-Bouquets. But he quickly discovered a beautiful camaraderie between the children and the dogs. He also noticed Aïda's kindness towards animals, and that she now had three close friends—more if you included little Jean-Zamor. Ludovic kept Ti Beau, Le Maître and Le Grand. He abandoned all thought of parting with the dogs, and today he raises them in much the same pedagogical spirit as he does the children.

*

Very well then, Ludovic Possible began the inventory of his library in storage shed. This helped the children to get accustomed to reading by organizing the books and identifying their content—an educational bargain. They could fabricate and erect a building dedicated to reading. They learnt what collaboration meant by moving wood and carrying various materials. Above all, they learnt to grasp the books, to hold them in their hands and smell them like the greatest kings and scholars on earth. Among them, Aïda knew as much about braiding thatch—and kicking and screaming at whomever pulled her hair—as she did about clearing swampy ground. She would soon enter puberty with a knowledge of reading, writing, fighting and counting. Yet nobody, whether in Boën or elsewhere, succeeded in teaching her how to speak, to use her words freely, either to chat idly or to ask the simplest questions.

This intermittent silence sculpted the contours of each of her words. Every sentence carried the potential to wound, for the simple reason of its rarity. Her words could thrill or unsettle, sow doubt or stir rancour even in the kindest conscience. Out of meanness, some locals would say that she was not like the others, that she was no ordinary child, 'No, no, of course, simpletons and retards are everywhere, so why not here? It's our turn!' they sneered. 'It's an epidemic. Their words vanish, and the children will forget how to speak. Soon, this new generation will only be able to communicate with hand gestures—no more words, no more language.' All of this because Aïda, far from being mute, searched for her words deep in the back of her throat, sometimes further still, into her soul—where her words found their precision and strength.

3

In the muggy cool of showers that yawned in the distance, but never arrived, it was Thursday. Like every Thursday evening, Papa Possible assembled all the plain had to offer—in terms of people in the twilight of life—for a game of dominoes. Without realizing it, he had created a ruling oligarchy of rough-and-ready village elders and guardians of moral order, almost as if he had established the 'Council of Notables' promised by the infamous rural code. Some came with decks of cards or musical instruments, while others, mostly women, aware of the commercial potential of such a gathering, set up their stoves and frying pans, and tables serving clairin and rhum arrangé, rum infused with spices and peels. A shot of grog here, a plume of tobacco smoke there, the evenings promised to be full of gossip interspersed with silences potent enough to decide everyone's life for them.

*

That night, Ludovic joined forces with Timoléon Jean-Baptiste to beat everyone else, a result not easy to accept, since Timoléon had given them such a hard time in his former life as a landlord.

Timoléon was the youngest of the group. His teeth had not yet come when the country was still known as Saint Domingue, and Black folks had to stare at the dust before their feet whenever they crossed paths with a white person. Let's just say, even after independence, Timoléon Jean-Baptiste had hardly lost his aggressiveness, his gift of the gab or his militant verve. He was known for his frequent bitterness and valiant defence of his interests as a farmer. In body and temperament, this man looked like he was carved from raw, unchanging nature. His scruffy beard was indistinguishable from his black face, for his hair and skin were of the same shade. His fingers had no phalanges, and you could barely tell the palm from the back of his rugged hands. His terrifying, massive paws gave the uncanny impression that he was preparing for a punch, as though his hands themselves threatened, independent of the rest of his body. And yet he could open his big mouth over his white teeth and let out words that were sensible, light and delicate. Timoléon was always seeking a master to fight, whether real or imaginary. Sometimes local farmers were not even aware that they had a problem until Timoléon revealed it to them with a simple gesture of reason. Once he pointed with his index finger, and the problem really came into being—half conceived, half resolved.

Timoléon Jean-Baptiste, the son of a revolutionary war veteran and the grandson—so he claimed—of an African king, had the looks of a truly courageous, newly initiated *nèg bosal*. With him by his side, Ludovic was not out of the woods yet—for, after a long sigh, Timoléon calmly placed his domino on the table and declared: 'I've challenged Balthazar to a duel. We've arranged the fight for Saturday afternoon.'

The silence fell again, as though everyone, picturing what Timoléon had just said, suddenly grasped the gravity of the next play. Around the table sat Alcius Louverture, also known as Brother Lélé, the spiritual one, a man who addressed his morning prayers to the four cardinal directions and who would not eat so much as the tip of a leaf without knowing who picked it, from where and under what conditions. Brother Lélé, everyone knows, organizes the nighttime dances and had made himself the guardian of the spirits. He initiated anyone who wished into the cults of the African gods and settled questions of kinship differently from Possible the Notary: in the realm of the disembodied worlds, parallel to and superimposed upon this one. He had shared his life, dating back to prehistory, with Mama Résia, a midwife and healer as devout as him in spiritual matters. The two were like peas in a pod. Also seated at the table was Bérénice Jean-Baptiste, Timoléon's neighbour, and the woman whom he credited for his beginnings as a soldier, back when he had been nothing but a poor farmer at the bottom of the agrarian pecking order, bound by the land-rent system and forced to sell high-priced goods in Croix-des-Bouquets in direct competition with the proprietors of the very soil he tilled. Bérénice and Brother Lélé did not even try to react to Timoléon's statement, knowing that the duel announcement was primarily addressed to Ludovic—the big boss, and the one most concerned with the life of Balthazar, the object of Timoléon's ire.

Balthazar Possible was Ludovic's half-brother—the youngest of his siblings, son of Father Possible. His birth was marked by the terrible occurrence of a death by spite, for—if it must be recalled—Ludovic's mother let herself die after learning that his father had acknowledged the child of a negro woman from the hills. She languished for six whole weeks in a sea of indignation and so on, as pointed out at the beginning of our story.

*

Before all this, long before what had just been said, the registries did not recognize Balthazar under the patronym Possible, like his father, but as Mouliez, the name of the plantation to which his maternal ancestors had belonged as personal property, *biens meubles*. After becoming Balthazar Possible, he was forced into a strange back-and-forth between a legitimate name and that of a bastard, and then from a bastard's name to yet another that hardly belonged to him. Call it a tricky notarial quandary —completely incomprehensible—but still a confusion which accorded Balthazar certain legal rights, and which underscored the implacable, well-rounded hatred between the two brothers. So much so that, if neither had yet passed on, it was partly driven by their expressed desire to outlive each other. The eldest held the youngest responsible for the death of his mother; the youngest held the eldest responsible for his father's denial. They hated each other for the nuances of their origins as much as their filial ties: one a mulatto-mulatto, the other a quadroon-mulatto, as though sullied by his negro mother.

Despite Balthazar Possible's advanced age, Timoléon Jean-Baptiste was well aware of his feats of arms, which alone discouraged him from seeking a quarrel. Balthazar had cultivated a gigantic corpulence beneath an intransigent jaw. His reputation for cruelty was so formidable that his very name could perform an exorcism, forcing evil spirits to flee. It was even invoked to force rebellious children to swallow their food. Balthazar Possible toiled all through his entire life perfecting his ill repute. Some land theft and seizures of goods are owed to him, apart from a certain form of expedient, automatic justice, characterized by the amputations ordered on a few actual—or suspected—thieves. Just two years ago, he buried a poor man to the waist, wrongly accusing him of stealing a goat from his land. After two days of martyrdom, Ludovic intervened—he dug the poor wretch out. Now unable to walk, not for any thievery—which he had not committed—but from the humiliation inflicted upon him, the man never set his dormant feet in the plain of Cul-de-Sac.

Balthazar had a fondness for such gratuitous demonstration of power and brute force. He was tolerated, enjoying an inviolable impunity born out of his social standing and of the fear he inspired. At the time when Ludovic still lived in Croix-des-Bouquets, visiting his lands and doling out orders like an *absentee colonist*, Balthazar was already settled in Boën and he spared no effort in organizing work, surveying the region, checking its sanitization and irrigation systems, from the sowing of seeds to the harvest, right down to hoeing and numerous other water-related operations. He also thought about securing the autonomy of the dwellings on the plain, another form of isolation that in turn protected them against the notorious *corvée* raging in the countryside: the population was seen as a reservoir of field hands that could be exploited to reduce *the debt*.

4

It was the thirty-eighth year of independence, or 1842 for the rest of the world. Sixteen years ago, the government in Port-au-Prince, then Port-Républicain, the titular capital of the Island of Haiti, Kiskeya or Boyo, from north to south, from east to west, had agreed to a financial debt to the country of France, following the implacable logic of paying recompense for its bygone servitude, including land and personal property.

Good King Charles the Tenth of France and Navarre set the sum of 150 million gold francs for what had been seized during the bloody anti-slavery and egalitarian revolution. He ordered the reimbursement of damages to the former metropole for the so-called unfortunate colonists, dispossessed by the Haitian movement. Having thrown off the yoke of oppression and founded a country, the former captives, maroon men and women, freed slaves, bosals born in Africa, Black Creoles born in the colony of Saint Domingue and everyone once classified by the Code Noir of 1685 as personal property, *biens meubles*, now learnt that they had to purchase their own bodies from the very owners they never accepted as such. Across the world, a singular consensus was spun around this affair: all the white countries—that is to say, every nation constituted on their terms and recognized by their standards, the powers of the world, big and small, imperialists and missionaries alike—quickly nodded in agreement with this excellent idea. The sole Black republic, the second independent country in the Americas after the United States, had to comply and pay up.

Since then, with this aim in mind, the very fine Jean-Pierre Boyer, the mulatto President-for-life of the entire Island of Haiti under the title of the Supreme Leader of the Nation, imposed drastic taxes on farmers, from north to south, from east to west —taxes that were often higher than the farmers' annual revenue. With such a ruinous system in place, the country not only reduced what folks call the *independence debt* but also ensured lasting poverty for generations to come. In order to sustain itself to carry out ambitious projects, to support industrialization, the Central Government drafted citizens into days of unpaid labour whenever it pleased. The corvée meant working your fingers to the bone all day long in exchange for a meagre survival diet at the worksite. Some willingly accepted, most of them soldiers. Others, pressured by armed troops, ultimately submitted.

There comes a time when intimidation no longer holds. When military pressure is protracted, it cracks from within. When abductions multiply across the country, you witness state dignitaries, urged on by their wives, ally themselves with popular movements, marching in Port-au-Prince and promising to sever the head and the neck from the President of the Republic's shoulders.

In such a context, Balthazar stayed true to his old habits. He had previously created a small, intermittent and unregulated tax ironically called 'the soldier's share', which he continued to distribute to the soldiers in Croix-des-Bouquets, greasing Commandant Éric Saurel's palms so that the countryside might be exempted from the census, remain invisible to tax collection and avoid the corvée roundups. As he demanded that Timoléon surrender his soldier's share, in either money or goods, Timoléon shouted back with no respect: 'About face, soldier! There's no more debt! There's a people's revolution!'

Only Balthazar's heart could measure the intensity of his vexation, such that it had contracted on itself. Seeing himself treated this way, almost for his own benefit, filled him with the bitter regret of aging—regret that he could no longer knock that bastard Timoléon's teeth out with his fist. He looked around, contemplating the kind of response that would be commensurate with the moral damage he had suffered. Then he understood what the finest jesters have always known: to mock someone, you must also mock yourself. Without thinking it through, he unbuttoned his trousers and took his time pissing on the cage of fighting cocks raised by his next-door neighbour, located in a corner of the yard. Balthazar spat, tucking away his flabby garter snake behind his courageous pleats, and left satisfied with his revenge, which only escalated the violence.

*

In the plain of Cul-de-Sac, the most exhilarating duels are the ones resolved by cockfights.

Since the cockfighting ring operated off the books, nothing that took place there could be judged in accordance with the law. The *gagè*, the cockfighting arena, and everything that surrounded it, was a juridical no man's land, a *terra incognita*. So much so that in the case of a fatal accident near the ring, Ludovic Possible would write down in his notebook: 'Location and cause of death: unknown to believers in Christ.' In other words, no human being worthy of the name could say where or how such a thing had happened. (Put otherwise, in parenthesis: the entire plain knew perfectly well what had happened, where and how it had taken place). Full stop. New paragraph. And so, immediately following the urinary affront, which Timoléon had observed with a tortured sense of calm, telling himself: 'Oh, so this is how it's going to be? Oh, is that right?' He picked up his champion among the landfowl, Biss the Undefeated, his massive and fearsome rooster with zero losses to his name, and marched with his shaggy goatee to the front of Balthazar Possible's yard. Standing stiffly, rooster tucked under his arms, he struck a soldierlike pose that bordered on ridiculous. 'Come out,' he grumbled, 'Come out at once!' He shouted whenever someone passed by, as if daring them to doubt his resolve. Two or three brays of a donkey later, still proud and satisfied with the effect of his eloquent urination, fully aware of his personal impact on the folks from Boën and beyond, Balthazar appeared on his verandah and hollered brazenly, pointing his chin towards Timoléon, 'Go home, poor dog, I will have plenty of time to decimate your shitty flock this Saturday afternoon.'

With this last retort, Balthazar once more revealed his dark side. He was feared and hated but also indispensable to the plain, especially because of his dealings with the army, which helped protect the fragile balance of this refuge. He was also known for looking after his lineage. Everyone in Boën knew how devoted he was to his grandchildren, and to their mother, his daughter Désirée. What folks did not realize is that Aïda's mother could also testify to this paternal devotion. Since the little girl had never known her father, Balthazar stopped by day after day to make sure everything was in order. At times he left a few centimes and some provisions—grain, a piece of ham—without asking anyone for anything or expecting thanks. Other times, he stuck around for a smoke, sharing a joint of tobacco from Aïda's mother's stash, which she gladly offered.

Ludovic Possible, for his part, no longer managed to properly orchestrate his domino matches in a way that might appease the feud. At the same time, by personal conviction, he was suspicious of the gagè and worried about the consequences of this cock-fighting business. He could not see how such a dual between a new friend and his perpetual enemy of a brother could amount to anything. The game clock ticked on without easing his sense of foreboding.

'I said go home, you oaf! Wait until Saturday to see what you've got coming,' Balthazar added.

The date of the great duel was set.

5

Even though protruding members are not characteristic of the avian species, Biss the Undefeated must have understood that the strange old man urinating on his comb bore no amicable feelings towards him. He must have sensed that this organ—so ugly and well hidden—was chiefly used for questionable tasks. For this reason or another, Biss was just as furious as his owner, the man whose honour he would defend that Saturday afternoon before all the peasants of the plain. After the schoolhouse for the children at Ludovic's, the cockfighting ring was the second-largest building in these parts. It served the bellicose needs of adults, hominids and landfowl alike, rather than the pedagogical needs of children. It was a rectangular gallodrome, accommodating numerous cages. At its centre stood a circular arena made of palm planks where folks hurled the poor beasts into the dust so they could brutally murder one another. Perhaps the beasts are not so poor after all, given their impatience to leap upon one another and peck their eyes out, even if they hadn't asked for it and had little to do with the invention of a practice that implicated them from the outset.

Nobody knows who invented cockfighting. Those who speak Spanish, living to the east on the other side of Lake Azuei, say that Cristoforo Colombo, their common ancestor, set foot in the Caribbean with a sword in one hand, the cross of civilization in the other, and a rooster tucked under his arm. A puzzling version, since every Spanish rooster was said to descend from this one, the superior specimen—besides which, they would have needed at least two to stage duels. Hence the English version, which insists that their fowl were drawn from the actual Indies, in Asia, and in sufficient quantity for cockfighting. Even their cousins, they add, could not resist importing birds to the vast territories of the North that they traded end-to-end in the US of A. To this day, the White House, from the first to its ninth and current resident, the tenth president of the United States, made no effort to hide their uncontrollable taste for poultry and bloody jousts, which corroborates the English version of events. However, nobody thought to ask the Native Americans for their opinion, even though they were here before. They have never stopped reminding everyone of the fact that they were here before. Perhaps in crossing the Bering Strait to populate this vast continent and its isles (many centuries before the arrival of the English, and long before the Spaniards), they were already accompanied by a few of these bellicose birds. Since, according to the Spaniards and the English, the birds in question hailed from the Indies—that is, if there is a difference between Indians and Indians—perhaps the practice of cockfighting was shared between the two, rather than by way of the English or the Spaniards. It seems that nobody, except the Indians, chooses to see things this way. Nonetheless, we still do not know who invented cockfighting. Unless the birds themselves devised their own game: an eternal vendetta, a secret to which nobody apart from them knows the answer.

*

Biss hardly asked himself any questions. He simply stood beside his cage, scoping out his adversary. None of this was of his own making, but he accepted his fate willingly, that is, to massacre his fellow birds. Biss was a rooster as massive and heavy as the fingers of his owner, Timoléon. His thighs were like those of an elder guineafowl. His imposing body afforded him a formidable ability to take a beating, but his prime asset lay in his surprising beak work. Since he was quite slow on his feet, his adversaries never anticipated such quickness when he turned his head to strike, snapping repeatedly like a viper. Biss was not called 'The Undefeated' just because it had a ring to it. For a few months now, he had dominated the plain's barnyards and gallodromes. Timoléon had received a lot of help in raising the bird as best as possible. Two years ago, he was the only one to spot Biss's tenacity. The rooster became a fine way for him to put to the test the national motto, *L'Union fait force*, strength in unity: he had Biss followed by his rooster friends, trained by various masters and competitively fed by his solitary comrades. In the end, the rooster embodied Timoléon's tenderness as much as the militant affection he attributes to collective labour.

The gagè was already full of supporters who heard that Timoléon challenged Balthazar to a duel. Some thought it was pure madness, others felt it was not yet time. Many could not believe their eyes. But everyone was there to witness the secret plan they had collectively concocted for this bird without saying it aloud: Biss had been training for two years with the sole intention of defeating one of Balthazar Possible's murderous roosters—

especially the rooster that was more legend than bird, the one they had given the macabre name of the Vile Beast.

In other words, the Vile Beast represented a kind of noise, a disembodied flapping of wings that stirred around the gagè. He terrified some and excited others. Some, without ever having seen Biss wage war, placed conditional bets so that their champion would not have to face such a phenomenon. Those who had already witnessed him in action were left dismayed by the violence displayed by such a small creature. Still, all his prowess was nothing compared to his reputation, which spread like wildfire from one village to the next, reaching even the walls of unknown cities. They said that the Vile Beast was no mere bird but two in one, his body reinforced by the power of a courageous man. They said that he did not go to sleep before nightfall, as is customary among the avian species. No! He would instead be engaged in acrobatic training routines after feasting on the bloody innards, freshly extracted from his foes. That was just the inner ring of gossip. Beyond that point, the rumours took on a kind of metaphysical eloquence. The Vile Beast was said to be an evil force of the great forests, as destructive as his master counterpart, ranked just below forest fires and hurricanes in May. It was worth asking whether this bird even needed people for his reputation to flourish, as much as they needed the Vile Beast to conjure their fantasies of devilish imps. This explained the general impression that folks were not ready for the imminent carnage, and, more than that, the paradoxical desire to push back an event that everyone wished would immediately unfold right before their eyes.

*

Before Balthazar arrived, an opening fight sowed chaos among the peasants and confirmed, in Ludovic's eyes, that an evil, warlike spirit had fouled the air people breathed in Boën. Doréus, his grandson, threw himself on top of his brother Jean-Zamor with a proven, yet surprising, tenacity for this age.

Doréus was a big-boned boy, a little oafish. He was one of Aïda's primary bullies, and Jean-Zamor constantly defended his friend against him. For a few weeks, since the little girl's body had begun to change, and since Doréus began to suspect new things about the lives of adult men, he had felt a growing need to inflict upon Aïda a particularly subtle form of cruelty. Something in his own body was troubling him, like a worm in his stomach. He swore that when he saw Aïda, the worm turned into a snake that snapped at his heart. So he gunned for her straight away, led by his guts and by a sensual, magnetic spitefulness.

It must be said that the gagè and the cockfights were a celebration for Aïda and her mother. As seasoned tobacco sellers, they saw the brown leaves go like hotcakes. Everyone knew the girl's mother. Aïda, invisible in the restlessness of the crowd, would be so engrossed in following the exchanges and hubbub that she at times forgot to charge people for the tobacco she delivered. She stood right there, her tray in hand, peddling her wares, not noticing that Doréus wanted to speak to her.

Aïda emerged from her stupor to the bustle of the two brawling brothers who punched each other with rabid violence as the adults tried to separate them. Jean-Zamor had just told Doréus: 'You pervert, can't you see she doesn't want to talk to you?' Doréus hurled himself at his younger brother as though by instinct, as though killing him would loosen the knots in his stomach.

Ludovic looked on, telling himself with disappointment that history, that bitch, only knew how to repeat itself, like the parakeets that the Hebraic and Mohammedan merchants carried on their shoulders to the great market in Croix-des-Bouquets.

Then Balthazar arrived.

Beneath his top hat, Balthazar wore a placid look, and he carried with him a single gamecock. A black sock had been shoved down to the winged gladiator's neck, leaving its beautiful tail feathers to arch in the wind.

*

So that he didn't have to make any arrangements, Balthazar brought along his bounty hunter and merchant friend, Luiz Hernando Santana, a mustachioed man from the East blessed with a joie de vivre so remarkable that they say he was always drunk on something. Luiz Hernando was raised in a family of sixteen girls, twenty-three boys and at least four children whose gender was unknown. They were all raised free-range on a farm with three *papás* and eight *mammás*, in such a way that, so as not to make anyone jealous or mistake someone's child for another's, the adults called all the children *Mi niño* or *Mi niña*, and, in return, they were called *tío* and *tía*, irrespective of their parentage. Luiz Hernando would tell you all of this while butchering whatever language he was speaking, including his native Spanish, laughing in your face and slapping on your shoulder, even if he had only learnt your name moments ago. While all his brothers old enough to fight enlisted in the factions opposed to the government in Port-au-Prince, demanding secession in the East, this Santana took pleasure in making friends throughout the West, selling gamecocks and vittles, and remaining vague about his political and ethnic leanings. One time, Balthazar asked him what he thought about the contestation in the Ozama, the south-east region of the country he hailed from, and he fetched the following answer, without straying from his infantile humour: 'Mira tío, you know I'd rather sell than separate.' Since then, they went about their business silently, without keeping score and without talking again about Ayiti's shifting geopolitics.

Luiz Hernando was interested in cockfighting as a pastime, which allowed him to put to good use his ability to identify the most ferocious animals when they were still young chicks. His real vocation, if he had one, was buying and selling anything that could materially change hands. He was only interested in business: he was in it as much for the spirit of the game as for the love of money. A merchant with every atom of his being, to Luiz Hernando people were not Black, white or mulatto—they were, first and foremost, buyers.

By bringing Luiz Hernando with him, Balthazar not only wanted to clear a handsome sum from the bets, he also wished to leave Ludovic—an easy target of his reprimands—baffled while he legitimately prepared to referee the afternoon duel. Luiz Hernando's presence would certainly trigger that reaction, given the known fact that Ludovic didn't want Santana the Dominican interfering with the business of the plain for much longer. In seeing Balthazar arrive with his accomplice, he realized the extent to which this arbitrage—this whole absurd matter of cockfighting to avoid, replace or provoke physical duels between two irritable men—should not exist, since no one seemed, at first glance, to have bad intentions.

Ludovic got up from his wicker chair, where he'd been sitting since noon, well before the arrival of the first spectators. He walked towards Timoléon, grabbed him by the arm and said:

'*Compère*, brother, you're a reasonable man. This time, let me pay the tax you wish to refuse. It'll be my last word.'

Since Timoléon announced, two days earlier, that he'd challenged Balthazar to a duel, Ludovic has tried in every way possible to dissuade him and postpone any reprisals. He tried everything he could from the height of his authority, but failed to even capture the attention of the two antagonists. Timoléon hardly paid Ludovic any mind; it was like complaining to a wall. Meanwhile, without much difficulty and in keeping with the diverging life lines on the palm of their hands, Balthazar made sure to avoid Ludovic altogether. So what was to come came about: the gamecocks tearing each other apart, with the folks around them not conducting themselves much better.

6

'Why is it that when the rooster crows its eyes are closed?'

'Because it knows all the notes to cock-a-doodle-doo by heart.'

The reason they introduce gamecocks to each other before subjecting them to battle is less of a joke. It's to see if they display any hostility towards the other, since nobody really knows what goes on in the minds of these little critters. In a distant moment in time, the time of storytelling, they observed beasts with strong reputations strike alliances as soon as they were set loose in the arena, avoiding the fight altogether. They even watched some birds rush to display their plump posteriors to their adversaries, eager to satisfy their shameful desires. It's the invention of the queer-cock, wanting to go wing to wing, their cloaca hoisted midair, an original behaviour highly detrimental to the murderous spectacle humans call for. In terms of spectacle, they now had an unspeakable one before their eyes: a psalmic battle pitting Biss the Undefeated against the Vile Beast.

Right after the presentation and the salutation between the two cocks, Biss scurried away to watch his formidable opponent move. He was skilled in close combat, in imposing the strength of his thighs and the quickness of his neck. But this time, he chose to keep his distance, staying on the defensive and observing the mode of attack the Vile Beast would launch. Faced with the choice among his many talents, the Vile Beast didn't begin aggressively either. Far from an ordinary fighter, he was—in a very different and much rarer way—the beast of all traits. Against a cock skilled with spurs—in this match the spurs were strapped into their heels—the Vile Beast became a deflector of talons, like in the human art of fencing. He parried blows and delivered attacks with mathematical precision. There was enough evidence, without any superstition, to speak of mastery and of a certain sang-froid. Against a more oafish adversary, who entered the arena like an irritated fool ready to land powerful strikes, he dipped with the wing and dodged without missing the chance to apply the full or partial strength of his own muscles. He would thrust his opponent against the walls of the arena, known as the round, using his advantage to throttle him. If you have a cock that doesn't attack foolishly, as the one now, that has instilled in itself a sense of hesitancy. This would be the first victory against a piece of work like the Vile Beast.

The sense of hesitation also gripped the spectators. It was not the same hesitation the cocks felt; it was tenser, like a sense of uncertainty that shifted from Balthazar's impatient gaze to Timoléon's restless fingers. The men, infuriated, had forgotten the basic principle of cockfighting—that adversaries never attack each other without first taking some time to think. Perhaps each of them judged the other's bird a worthless opponent—a thought rooted in bad faith.

*

Old Ludovic was the only one to remain calm. He gathered that Luiz Hernando had no role in this fight other than to collect the bets placed by the assembled peasants. He had no clue how well it suited Luiz Hernando, who at that moment was on the verge of an oral orgasm prompted by the many wads of bills he was counting in both hands. Interrupted each time by his own smile, he could not stop licking his lips. This was no longer just a tooth gap; this slot between his two upper incisors had become an open passageway to his good spirits. Luiz Hernando was in his element. He announced a substantial bet of two gourdes. Once the call for bets was over, any farmer who could not line up seven well-counted gourdes was denied a counter-stamped seal with the initials of his champion. Santana also seized the opportunity to increase the amount of fees withheld, which went from fifteen to fifty centimes per bet. At the call of *no more bets*, when they finally tossed the gamecocks into the round, he had a confiscatory yet luminous idea: for the peasants who wanted to gamble during the fight, he said that the only way to place new bets was to purchase a bet already in progress. That is, a gambler and an interested party could strike down a new transaction. If the gambler was pleased with his champion, he could sell his bet up to three times the sum of the money in stake; if he was no longer comfortable with his choice, he could cede half of his initial bet. And don't forget the fees! No longer were they fifty centimes per bet but one solid, beautiful gourde nationale for every change of hand. A system that promised to be fruitful, since the two beasts in the arena were each at once odds-on losers and favourites. It was a no-spurs-added fight, and the severity of the blows made it impossible to imagine that either of the birds would ever tire.

The battle is hard fought. Having finally attacked first, Biss positioned himself in front of the Vile Beast as though he was accustomed to training his cabrioles. He wore his feathers short and imposed his style of combat—sober and deliberate. Completely confident, the Vile Beast knew that he could leap much higher than his opponent, so he tried to cut through to reach the back of Biss's neck. This was no easy feat since, with every leap, Biss pivoted just in time and found a way to block his formidable adversary, giving the impression that the vile bird was trying to flee the ring. After a few jabs, the Vile Beast remembered that he was also allowed to fight like a boxer. He set himself against the rails of the ring and offered the spectacle of an Olympic brawl. The two beasts hardly jumped now as they tried to tear each other's eyes out. Meanwhile, the humans outside the ring, dazed by the fight, brayed with the confused goal of either cheering their champion or toppling his opponent. Among them, only two did not behave like the others: Balthazar grabbed his chin with one hand and twisted it in bewilderment, while Timoléon, partially satisfied, kept dripping the handle of his pruning knife with his thick fingers, muttering: 'Yeah, that's it, that's it,' like a mirror image of the time before, when his enemy had pissed over the heads of his roosters.

*

At the height of the carnage in the arena, Ludovic called time —long enough to clean wounds with bitter oranges, to spew alcohol mixed with saliva on the birds' thighs, and, who knows, to announce a few instructions to each opponent for the next round of hostilities. An interlude like this proved providential not only for the battered gamecocks but also for the boiling crowd in the arena. Bets were bought and sold in a kind of speculation unknown to this rural plain. Folks made the most of the timeout by downing a few glasses of tafia, rolling a joint of tobacco or relighting their pipes. They brayed at the top of their lungs as the sweat traced a path from the veins in their necks to the collar of their shirts. They laughed and traded ridiculous wisecracks about the outcome of the fight.

Music began to play. A banjo tune accompanied by a raspy voice, labouring to pierce the thick mass of testosterone saturating the air. The cockfight resumed in no time, and the birds seemed to have forgotten that they had already met—and that they despised each other. They clashed again with renewed hostility.

This time, the Vile Beast was more restless, nearly retreating from battle. Biss lunged forward; the Beast jumped and dodged. Biss struck again; the Beast ducked by turning his back. This went on a few more times. They traversed all four metres of the arena, and while they were at it, Balthazar let out a big, awful laugh. Then he suddenly stopped. At this instant, the Vile Beast turned on Biss the Undefeated with such violence it seemed worthy of inclusion in a sacred text.

He launched a savage attack on Biss's left eye. Blood spurted, and Biss started turning to only one way, as though bewildered—why, all of a sudden, could he see only half the crowd. The Beast soon reminded everyone why the word 'Vile' was part of his name. Instead of attacking the right eye, which would have spelled victory, the Beast returned to attack the same eye, pecking at it again, followed by two heel kicks to the side of the neck, and on the left side, aiming to paralyse that half of Biss the Undefeated's body. The result was clear and decisive. Biss opened his left wing to steady his faltering balance, to keep a safe distance and to attack only from the right. The Vile Beast noticed, and circled him. Those who know Balthazar Possible would recognize in this small winged creature the same desire to humiliate that sometimes drove his arrogant master. Now, the Beast no longer fought with passion or quickness. He strutted about, striking with his wings and beak. Each time the newly blinded Biss's raw aggression pushed him to react, the Vile Beast answered with even greater force, just enough to boast. At last, the Beast delivered the fatal blow below the neck. Biss the brawler could no longer pick himself up. He drew back his thighs and, to the crowd's astonishment, breathed his final breath.

*

As everyone knows, defeathering the losing bird is a right reserved for the victorious trainer. Just as Balthazar stepped forward to collect his spoils, Timoléon cut him off and clutched his champion, cradling him as though he were shielding from a sudden draught. This was the beginning of an insult. Some farmers were still talking over the fight, while others were already taking front-row seats for the next round. In his heart of hearts, Timoléon did not merely cherish the collective labour that Biss the Undefeated embodied—the rooster was an extension of himself. Even though no words could express the singular love he felt for the bird, he was compelled to say something meaningful over its remains, to speak on behalf of the entire plain of Cul-de-Sac. Perhaps he felt that none of this—the cockfights, the gambling, the uproar, the sweat and dampness—was truly necessary at the end of the day. But he had no time to pour his heart out because his adversary was already there to claim his due. Under Ludovic Possible's watchful eye, he surrendered the bird. Balthazar immediately tore it from his arms and, instead of keeping it as a trophy, hurled it to the ground, trampling it, spitting on it, trampling it again, then kicking it one last time. Just as he looked up from this outrageous scene, Balthazar saw his own cock beneath Timoléon's right arm as the man brandished his pruning knife. He barely had the time to let out a wild shriek before Timoléon severed the poor Vile Beast's neck from its body, its arteries pissing thin streams of black blood.

The terrible afternoon burned on. The sun broke from behind the hills like the bursting of a yellow fruit, spewing its golden juice all over the sombre clouds on the horizon. It was exactly six o'clock.

7

Time is grave—it has been raining for twenty-four hours. The rain that yawned in the distance has finally arrived. At first, fine droplets wafted in the wind. Then bursts of rain came hurtling down on the thatch and tiles, the wind whistling between the shutters and door panels. The rain is good for the lime-washed walls, leaving no cause for worry. Folks might even have rejoiced, had the events at the cockfighting ring not stained these gusts with a strange, foreboding hue. It is the familiar rain that washes over the bitterness of men, as though it had sought out their lives, pouring down as the tensions rise.

*

This masculine, brutal and now sodden world also belongs to little Aïda. Beyond what she grasped during her adventures at Master Possible's home, she learnt from her mother how to sow seeds, harvest crops, tend and watch over them and gather brown tobacco leaves. Having devoted herself to this art since the age of reason, she has become an active participant, especially in the last two years, during which she has worked the whole cycle, from seeding to sale: harvesting, drying and infusing the leaves.

These activities root Aïda firmly into the Boën community. And as with everyone else, the day's tensions weigh on her tonight.

Aïda is in a closed room. The room is too small, the walls are too close, far too close. They close in. They try to corner her, crush her, swallow her whole. As the walls press tighter, Aïda starts to suffocate. Push Aïda, push! The walls are closing in. Close your eyes, Aïda! Keep pushing, save yourself! She tries not to look, not to think of the walls devouring her. She searches for a sliver of strength—it swells, bubbling, crowding at the back of her throat. Suddenly she lets loose, bellowing, screaming with all the strength she has left. Aïda pushes with the strength of her cry. She howls at the top of her lungs. Her whole body is caught in the scream. Aïda cracks the walls that trample her. She wails, surpassing the power of her own voice. She breaks through, freeing herself. Now she's free. Now she is alone. Aïda tears down the walls, liberating herself. She wakes with a jolt.

Her mother, more accustomed to waking Aïda at night than being awakened by her, interpreted recent events and thought there was more than met the eye, and none of it was good. The two brothers feuding, the cockfight, the rain—all had seeped into the dreams of her only child. Outside, the evening poured, lashing on soil, plants and insects. On the mat beside her mother's bed, Aïda trembled under her covers. Her mother was not faring well either: her coughing had worsened, and her breathing troubles were accompanied by deep, repetitive hiccups. She climbed out of bed to check on her daughter. Leaning against the frame, she cradled the child between her legs, keeping them both warm in the dark, wrapped in the roar of the thunderous storm. She wanted to speak to her as a friend, to tell Aïda one of the many stories her daughter had always listened with eyes wide open, as though her very existence depended on it.

*

Aïda's mother told her her first story on the night she was conceived. When the man pulled himself out of her and abandoned her in bed in the darkness to gallop home to his wife, more hurried than usual, Aïda's mother already felt pregnant. She placed a hand on her lower abdomen and told her fertile ovaries the very first story she'd learnt from her own mother, who had learnt it from her grandmother, who had learnt it from her great-grandmother, from her ancestor, great-grandmother and great-great-grandmother and so on, all the way to the Gulf of Benin, where her foremothers passed down the magical gift of the chanted and recited word, from woman to woman, since the creation of the world forever and ever.

In the place where they all came from, so goes the story, there was a kind of woman between a *sirène* and a human, between a goddess and a woman, poised to enchant a crowd with the gentle power of her voice. She was a chantrèl, a singer admired by the rich and the poor alike. She would sing and lift herself above the crowd. When she spoke, things happened. When she made demands, people set to work. With her voice, the rapture she stirred caused men to fear for their own sanity. This was the story of the true chantrèl women. These women were nothing like those left behind in some forgotten corner, dusted off on occasion for the span of a dance accompanied by drums and bugles during harvest festivals, or for funerals. This was the story of the real queens, their song adorned with lyrics and rhythm embedded in every fibre of their being. This was the eternal legend of the chantrèl queens, samba women, women griots, female fabulists to whom the land of Africa, Olohoum himself and all the gods of the Vodou pantheon gifted the word for centuries upon centuries, wherever they may have found themselves and no matter their age.

Since the telling of this initiatory parable, and over the years, Aïda's mother's heightened reality has allowed her daughter to dream. For, at this point of the story, she is the only woman who sings during critical moments. For example, the other night during the break in the cockfight, it was her voice that rose above the banjo's tune. She is certainly appreciated for it, and sometimes she is even asked to sing on her own. But it is hard to imagine the chantrèl queen as a superior race of diva; this revealed her one and only literary intention: to encourage her daughter to apply the brushstrokes of language to life and make greater use her words. This could have worked, since Aïda never lost interest in her mother's stories. Whether they were the most familiar tales, passed down from mother to daughter since the old days of ancestral Ginen, the story of a newly invented marvellous hero, or even the more personal story of her unknown father—magnificent, but never the same in each telling. Aïda always welcomed the latest unexpected twists and turns, nurturing them deep inside herself to shield her from the madness around her. The stories protect her from great disturbances: the cockfighting ring, the duels, the inclement weather or the recent events that saw the Vile Beast relieved of his head and Balthazar, its master, lose his own in a whirlwind of threatening insults.

*

Two men came together to hold Balthazar Possible, even though he was not struggling. Before Balthazar let out that wild scream, just as he was about to witness Timoléon Jean-Baptiste's brazen crime, Agonan the musician dropped his banjo and rushed to him, as did Gibril Cador, his brother-in-law and companion to his daughter Désirée. They held Balthazar back as he fought to suppress his blistering reaction. You could see it in the way the veins in his neck swelled, in the tightening of his jaw, in the drool that bubbled at the corner of his lips. Balthazar let out the shriek of a wounded cat, his whole body trembling, before declaring that if they released him, he would kill, one by one, all those he believed had allowed Timoléon near his fallen champion, beginning with that bastard, Papa Possible. He was not released, of course. Gibril Cador and Agonan, aided by a few peasant women in pursuit of peace, dragged him into the torment of his home.

At home, sitting alone behind the grand table, in a darkness hardly disturbed by an oil lamp, Balthazar saw the rain coming. A tangle of feelings arose, filling his entire body. For him, his Vile Beast was not a creature for fighting and gambling. The proud performances of the rooster disguised the fragility that bound them together. The Vile Beast and Balthazar loved each other as much. He sat unflinching, a cold and empty void growing within—more dizzying than painful—that might easily have filled with burning hatred. But instead of hatred, only regret for the loss of his proud gamecock welled up. And since Balthazar is who he is and cannot act otherwise, the harder he tried to loathe, the more insistently regret pressed in on him, even stirring the desire to shed tears. In the end, he resented Timoléon not for murdering his beautiful bird but for depriving him of his hatred. From this regret he drew, finally, the strength to loathe once more, in a colder, more calculated way than before.

Elsewhere, his friend Luiz Hernando Santana was never overwhelmed by emotion, and he never lost sight of his accounts. As Balthazar was led out before his eyes, escorted out by force, he took the time to complete the last of his transactions. Some peasants lost more than they possessed and others won more than the bogus business of cockfighting could ever yield. The accounts had to be balanced by debts and promissory notes, words of honour and a few *mèsi konpè*'s—thank you, my brother—all certain to guarantee that the plain's more serious problems were yet to come. When he was done, Hernando noticed the storm approaching. He chose to spend the night with Balthazar, suspecting the rain had no intention of leaving any time soon.

8

Two days later, after the rude awakening and a long day of silence, indifferent to the disruption of time itself, Aïda's mother started to braid her daughter's hair. On the verandah, perched between her mother's legs with her head down, the little girl searched for a sense of calm. Soon, she could no longer feel her mother's fingers in her hair, nor hear her mother's slight and serious voice, nasal and ravaged—the one she loved the most. Her mother had paused long enough to take a strong dose of snuff up her nose and let out a deep cough. Aïda preferred it when her mother smoked tobacco rather than inhaled it. She liked watching her light a pipe or a joint dangling in the corner of her beak. What she disliked about snuff was that the act of stuffing one's nose seemed the very image of submission: you had to bend down and hide your face, and the cough that followed came like a punishment. But turning your head to the side, drawing your mouth to a flame, taking a pull and letting go—Aïda told herself, certainly in her own words—carried an air of audacity, elegance, even defiance. It was the only time she saw her mother reign supreme over something, even if it was nothing more than her own breath.

It was the night before market day. Nowhere was it written that the daily bread would come from the bars of tobacco powder they offered the marketgoers. Still, there was something quite beautiful about doing up your daughter's hair so you could take her along, a basket on your head, to haggle over two more centimes with penniless peasants. Before the market, the two would fall asleep in the sullen, familiar calm of a fatherless home—Aïda's spirits lifted, her mother's tender.

*

A few hours later, with the arrival of a subdued sunrise, the mother's coughing fit awoke the daughter. Aïda brought the vase and the basin of water. This morning ritual began with even more pain than the week before. Aïda's mother tried to pull herself from her stiff bed. She could not. It was as though her covers had suddenly grown heavier, while her stomach churned with the cold cough rising from her throat. She coughed and hacked, as if trying to repel the invisible hand clenching her trachea. The talons held fast, letting out only a few clumps of greenish yellow phlegm streaked with blood into the white vase, more intense and visible this morning.

Time flows on, making all things possible. Aïda's mother managed to wrest herself from the grip of pain, and here they were, standing at the market despite the rain, eight stone's throw from home, earlier than necessary, hoping life had more to offer them today than what lay ahead in the days to come. Rain poured so heavily from the sky that it didn't fall in drops but in buckets, begging the question: what would the snakes that couldn't swim or the infant frogs do? These tiny creatures always managed somehow. Born of the earth, knowing all its nooks and crannies, they seemed to cope better in Noah's day, than the great vertebrates who rule the world, humans chief among them, not even able to begin their market day as planned.

Look at these market women, their hair drenched in the perennial sadness of a rain that let nothing escape its path. They were soaked to the root, their heels sunk deep in the mud. The soil had turned to mud, melting away, and their wares would soon be wasted. Yet the hardiest among them, having travelled far, lingered through part of the day, battered by the showers, seeking shelter here and there under shacks made of palm leaves.

For now, they accepted their destiny. Nature's outburst would claim the best of their weekly labour. A morsel of bread for four centimes, *mèsi konmè*—thank you dear, see you next time. They endured the misfortune of Tapage Market's proximity to the White River, which, spilling over in fury, unleashed one of its dormant tributaries to engulf a large portion of their goods.

What the devil were they to do in this mayhem? The poor market women fought like a closed fist against the elements, not to save their provisions and bread, essential oils, chocolate balls, fruits, vegetables or meat, but to return safe and sound, home or elsewhere, preferably with their livestock and before the worst of the deluge. And so, on this rainy evening, the population of every home in Boën doubled, driven by the overflowing river and in keeping with the fundamental, universal and inalienable rules of generosity. Yes, indeed! Each household welcomed one or two people who were complete strangers, without asking how much longer life would be measured in freshwater and worries.

9

Home alone, seated at his dinner table, Ludovic Possible assessed the damage. The duel kept its sinister promise of strife, and the weather turned foul. Through the open panel of the front door, he saw a delicate rain jostled about by the wind. The wind and the rain seemed as if they had always been there, swaying immutably behind the door panels. Suddenly, a huge bolt of lightning tore open the tender skin of the sky. Ludovic, the poor devil, felt his heart pounding like a drum. He felt like his insides were failing. He could no longer endure such shocks and wished to escape the loneliness of his home. If not for the delicate rain, he would have stepped onto the verandah, sat with his legs crossed, and clasped his right shoulder with his left hand in the comfort of his majestic chair. This posture lent him the image of a leader, setting aside certain worries and granting him haphazard reassurance. There he would await visitors and gossip. He often received farmers in kind of a role-reversal ritual, where the peasants seemed obliged to do him all manner of favours. Yet, as he was painfully aware of in the present moment of complete isolation, it was he who needed the Boënnais and their neighbours. He understood the madness of living here all alone in the twilight of his days. From time to time, the thought came to him that nobody could make up for lost time, that he risked causing further harm by trying to make amends for past mistakes. Perhaps it was the best, he told himself, to let the children to grow up without intrusions into their lives made in the name of education for all, and of a shared future.

Aïda was the one who interested Papa Possible the most. But he did not have the fortune to be part of her tight-knit circle of friends. Yet, despite her silence—or perhaps because of it—Aïda remained a pleasant child. Jean-Zamor made her smile. The three dogs—Ti Beau, Le Maître and Le Grand—amused her. She would encourage them to run around and play with one another. And the animals seemed to particularly enjoy her peaceful company.

Aïda counted two other friends at Tapage Market: Désirée Possible, with whom she would have dinner when her mother was away, and the explosive Paloma Placide, once known as Pépé the Tempest because of her initials and her reputation—whom her friends called Cousine Palo.

At Tapage Market, as in their lives, Paloma Placide is a point of pride for Aïda and her mother. Pépé was what they called a superb woman, exuding a spectacular orchestra from every part of her being. She was not usually in Boën; she came only to ensure the proper running of her affairs: the various businesses she entrusts to a corps of market women. Along the way, she exposed herself to the jealousy of her rival women and the desire of men—something she was not altogether happy about. A prolific talker and majestic queen, Paloma lived in Croix-des-Bouquets and welcomed the company of anyone and everyone:

the district commandant, the division general, the parishioner on a mission, the respected travelling merchant looking for a place to set up shop. They said that, if necessary, even the Supreme Leader himself, the military president-for-life of the first and only Black republic in the world, would call on Pépé to visit with his troops, for if they squeezed in tight, all three hundred inhabitants of Boën could fit into Paloma Placide's massive house, a sophisticated Victorian gingerbread that was the spitting image of abundance.

*

Cut off by the rainfall that left them stranded at Tapage Market, Aïda and her mother were seeking refuge at the home of Désirée and her compère, Gibril Cador, when they stumbled upon the magnificent Paloma Placide.

Thirteen years earlier, when Aïda was still in the womb, Pépé first told Aïda's mother that she wished to become the child's mother. She announced her intention in the third month of her pregnancy. Upon learning of the disavowed paternity of the unborn child, Pépé showed up in the yard beneath the tobacco factory and said to the mother, 'If you give me this baby, commère, I assure you that the two of us will be mothers, from beginning to end.' Aïda's mother offered no reply. Pépé allowed herself to add, in her muffled voice, 'Cousine, this child is going to need someone else . . . please . . . you have no idea how much I need this.' Since then, she has never ceased to reiterate her request in every possible way—sometimes in jest, sometimes with the utmost seriousness. So much so that, although Paloma is supposedly Aïda's godmother, the child was never allowed to visit her residence in Croix-des-Bouquets, for the mother feared that Paloma might sequester her there for life.

Still, there reigns a certain compromise between Aïda's mother and Cousine Palo, which allows her to fulfil her role as aunt or godmother without the title. When she comes to the vicinity, Pépé always brings something for Aïda. Thanks to her, before the little girl could even speak, she had learnt that one could give or receive something not essential for survival, for food or clothing, but something like a drawing, a figurine, a doll, a set of jacks or a little bird made of wood that will never sing. The charm of these trifles enacted a maternal exchange whenever Paloma was in Boën. She did the child's hair, followed her about, cajoled her, not to mention that she told her stories and sang songs—very different from those of Aïda's true mother. For Paloma was not a renowned chantrèl, lacking the ancestral gift of words passed down from generation to generation, carried all the way from Afrique-Guinée in the holds of the slave ships to the fissured lands of the Americas. Paloma was also a powerful woman in her own way, able to enliven a crowd with her voice. By the grace of respect and firm social standing, she came to be recognized as a sort of a chantrèl—without the tradition.

Paloma Placide was visiting Gibril and Désirée when she saw her so-called cousin and niece arrive completely soaked. She opened her arms wide and exclaimed:

'Something must be done!'

She said it in such a way that one could not tell if she was speaking of the present deluge or the pathetic state of her two protégées.

*

At the other end of Boën, the White River quit her bed and went in search of arable soil. She meandered towards stables, yards, plantations and garden plots, intent on flooding the lives of humans, their houses, even their tombs; spilling farther still, forcing herself wherever her waters could wreak the most havoc. In ordinary times, the river is conscious of trees and people. Her waters followed their course, nourishing the lands, carrying crustaceans and a few small green snakes, sometimes causing droughts here and there, but limiting its whims to a change in course or mild overflows. For this alone, the farmers called the White River hardheaded, difficult to bend. Her flow stopped precisely when they needed it the most, no amount of cajoling could change her mind. She would retreat deep beneath the earth's surface, or remain lurking in her bed of fresh stones high up in the hills. At such times, the farmers managed however they could. Some dug drainage systems, others forged ponds.

Sometimes Brother Lélé, the self-proclaimed guardian of the spirits, would pay the White River a visit. He brought with him a few other devotees in obeisance of the spirits and ritual practices. Those from Mardelle—oh so belles! And from Peyrac—they arrived as a pack! All the way from O'Gorman, each and every one! One came from Juan, fainting from the sun! And like an anthill, they came from Vaudreuil! These mystical agents from across the region organized pilgrimages to the source of the White River, with libations and prayers.

'Something must be done!' Pépé the Tempest declared, for this deluge was no simple matter. Death was at the doorstep.

10

The weather had settled.

Bérénice Jean-Baptiste, Timoléon's companion, woke up early in the morning and went to open one of the panels of the front door. She heard something scratching the other side. She hesitated, then pulled it open. She found herself face to face with a strange creature: a gigantic blind rooster, the size of a grown man. She let out a piercing scream, woke up again, went to the front door, opened it, and once more found herself in front of the ignoble creature. She tried to calm herself, waking up *for real* this time beside Timoléon Jean-Baptiste—who had dreamt the same dream, except for one difference: the rooster that he had seen had its head to its neck, exposing a bloody gash. Timoléon had kept this dream to himself for almost two weeks since he had decapitated the Vile Beast. Now that Bérénice had the same dream and he thought of sharing the news with her people, we would soon learn that this nightmare was lurking everywhere around the plain. What occurred in one's sheets was a private matter, not to be told, yet it so marked the night that, come morning, everyone recounted their evenings while carefully avoiding to mention of what they had dreamt.

Bérénice is not a woman of the Cul-de-Sac plain. She comes from the city. She can read and write in fine script, and she fought wherever she could against the confounding logic that barred people from entering the joyous circle of modernity with wide open arms. It has already been fourteen years since she met a young peasant learning the ways of politics. She took him under her wing and then, shortly after, decided to indulge the eternal urban fantasy of returning to nature. After years of peasant life with Timoléon, after three miscarriages and the loss of two children, Bérénice had not lost hope of reversing the colonial order—that is, the end of mulatto rule—without replacing it with some God-knows-what Black aristocracy. For the time being, her contribution to this future world of love and peace, free of domination and ethnic strife, was limited to cajoling an excessively exuberant companion, wishing to bear him more sweet children, and, above all, spreading the good word of education and science wherever the opportunity arose. This is why Ludovic Possible had once found in her a solid ally for his own educational efforts.

*

Bérénice and Timoléon lived a stone's throw from Papa Possible. All they had to do was exit the notary's front yard, take a few steps to their left, pass the mango trees no one ever touched, and walk past the little path on the right bordered by sugarcane that led to Tapage Market. Further down, to the right, two coconut palms were rooted inside the yard of the two liveliest political minds in the entire plain. Thanks to this proximity, the notary did not solely have a schoolhouse and children to occupy his time. Bérénice managed the house, brought order to the day, and furnished a sense of presence to all around her. It was she, for example, who suggested involving certain parents in the children's instruction.

The same geographical propinquity also explained why Timoléon Jean-Baptiste never skipped a round of dominoes on Thursday evenings. The complicity that was established between these men eventually subsumed the tensions that had once seemed essential to Timoléon's vision of the world. When Ludovic lived far away, he was merely profiting from the labour of lowly peasants. Now that he was present in the flesh and alliances could be forged, the personal took precedence over the political.

Meanwhile, in these long rainy days, as we withdraw into ourselves, we set our demons free: the bourgeoisie and the people share the same dread. They endure the same troubled sleep and ultimately dream of the same gigantic rooster scratching at the door, waiting for us to fall back into slumber, scratching again and again, until the final rude awakening.

*

Bérénice came to tell Papa Possible about her dream. Seated in front of his visitor, the patriarch sipped his morning coffee without once thinking to offer her a cup. He did not reach for his notebook—a Moroccan leather folio he would have opened for anyone else. Bérénice was never party to those visits where townspeople insisted on telling him everything. Ludovic rested his right arm on the table and rocked back and forth, calm and attentive. Outside, the rain was so fine that it could scarcely be seen. In such circumstances, people did not come seeking pleasure or just to say 'Oh yes, I dreamt of this or that.' Bérénice and Ludovic were reaching a new state of intimacy, and they knew it. She began her story with her first awakening: the door panels, the latch, the scratching on the other side. Ludovic quickly completed the story: the discovery of the gigantic rooster, the reawakening, the door panels, the latch, the scratching, the rooster reappearing in the same spot. He, too, had the same dream.

Bérénice was a woman full of rational assurance—it was her specialty. She believed that the gods of Africa alive in Haiti are nothing more than nostalgia and consolation, that the one and only god, if he exists, has nothing to do with humans, and that all magic, good or evil, only worked if one chose to believe in it. Yet, in these circumstances, her rational assurances were blown to smithereens. Although she resisted drinking from the absinthe of the supernatural, Bérénice felt at home here in the plain of Cul-de-Sac during these moments when reason was put to the test. A fascination, a philosophical astonishment, as though she had touched the flesh and blood of something that was nothing less than the profound soul of this place.

Ludovic could tell she was confused. He was no less so; he was, in fact, completely lost.

'What shall we do?' Bérénice asked.

He had no clue. He did not even know if anything was truly wrong. And if there was, what exactly was the problem all about?

He accompanied his commère to the verandah, watched her leave and saw her walk further away, carrying on her shoulders the invisible weight of the most perfect mystery. Ludovic went back inside, sat down for a few moments, and thought of nothing in particular. Then he stood up and returned to the verandah. He looked out at the horizon—soon he would have to survey the house, the hamlet, the countryside, to mark what must be buried and what rebuilt. Inside once more, he felt the spiritual need to pour out three drops of fresh water on the ground. He opened his cupboard and pulled out a white enamelled goblet with a black handle. But when he opened the side door to perform the libation, he realized that he knew neither the ritual gestures nor a single expiatory phrase. He suddenly saw himself for what he was: a small-town Christian, a bourgeois mulatto, with no idea how to speak to the wind and the earth. He stopped, lifted the goblet to his nose and inhaled the sweet odour of the fresh water. A sliver of shame kept him from drinking the water that was meant for a simple ritual that he did not know how to perform. He placed the full goblet on the table and decided, without further ado, to go see Alcius Louverture, Brother Lélé, who surely knew better than he did.

*

The foul weather left the plain stripped bare, all skin and bones. Certain paths had become little more than mud tracks, where one could barely distinguish garden plots from the verges. Many heads of livestock were lost, including a donkey belonging to Désirée and Gibril. He was named Gabriel, peace unto his soul, and was the brother of a rescued donkey called Satan, who had been named for his black coat and for the way he mistreated Gabriel from birth. A few human corpses were also unearthed, though they had died long before the deluge: the waters swept away at least eight of the twenty-four occupied tombs that bordered Boën, and severely damaged several others, including the one that awaited Ludovic Possible himself, thirty metres behind his yard, next to his schoolhouse. When he arrived in Boën, Ludovic had his house renovated, and, to ensure that he would spend the rest of his days there, he decided to have a two-part tomb erected. The bitter aftertaste of which he felt today, as he exclaimed, 'Well, damn! I thought I wasn't long for this world!' Ever since the deluge and destruction, he has been saying to anyone who will lend an ear, 'I'm going to die. I shall repair my tomb, and then I'll be off.'

There were uprooted trees, bulbs wrenched from the soil, pigeon peas, peppers, shallots, corn—the entire season lost. Two bowers remained, their names the only trace—the cockfighting ring and the school. Everything would require much effort to repair, goods to reproduce, large sums of money that the peasants did not possess—a debt to the earth. This, in addition to the made-up debts and criminal indictments they owed to Port-au-Prince and France, accounted for the devastation in their minds, causing them to have nightmares of animal slaughter—the foretelling of collective insanity.

Only Aïda's mother was spared the lonely nights. Her suffering kept her from dreaming of bloody roosters. Her nights were long and her internal passageways, her bronchial tubes and trachea, were the source of acute pain. Fortunately, Paloma had decided to stay for a few more days, since poor Aïda, helpless as she was, could only offer her mother a little water to drink and lament her pain. Cousine Palo proved to be a source of help and comfort. She prepared tinctures, made sure there was daily sustenance, and called the entire plain's attention to the mother's plight.

*

Before the rain had completely ceased over the countryside, Brother Lélé told Ludovic that what had to be done, dear friend, was to bring all of the townspeople together in a procession—one great prayer addressed to the wind, the trees, the sun, the mountains, the river, and every being that draws breath in this world and others. Ludovic was not expecting such a radical prescription, but having felt himself the tender desire of sanctification, he could only acquiesce. And so, there we had it: Brother Lélé, Mama Résia, Paloma and Aïda's mother supported by her daughter, all at the vanguard of a collective, solemn gesture. By the dozens, peasants emerged from their homes across Boën and beyond, dressed in white and asking themselves how they would save these vestments from the muddy mess that the plains had become.

They came without a word, their feet bare, following one another, tracing the bank of the river. They moved towards the headwaters, as if they were going to the source of it all. Everyone brought something: an enamel cup, a lit candle weary from its future in the humid air, half a calabash, a jug filled with drinking water, a rosary, a banner of some unknown nation, a bottle of clairin, a goblet of wine, three little pots, seven rooster crests, a small green chair. For fifteen days, they had to implore, pray, call upon and exhort the mistresses of the waters, the gods of the heavens and the earth. For fifteen days, they pleaded with the forces that command the oceans, the seas, the streams and rivers and every source that swells from the earth, in the mountains and on the plain. For fifteen days, while showers rained down with gusts of wind on the poor Christian souls, they asked Papa Loko, spirit of the fiercest winds and of the slowest knots of air, of typhoons, tropical storms and hurricanes: 'Papa Loko, please, go seek Agwe, Agwetawoyo, Agwe twa fwa, guardian of the seas, go seek the sirène, the hydra of fresh water, bèt-sèt-tèt, every blade of grass beneath the waters, every puff of clouds in the sky. Go seek, go speak, tell them that it is enough for now, the debt is paid. Go seek, go speak, tell them that the White River can hear no more, twa fwa, tell them thrice, the saints, the angels, the demons, those passing through. Eternal Father, Great Keeper, Olohoum, go seek, go speak, gods of the heavens, of all the nations of the earth and the other worlds, goddesses past, present and future, for all the time that has been, that is, that ever will be. Go seek, go seek, seven times, seventy-seven times seven.' Then, a breakthrough: a greater clarity and an unravelling of the clouds. At Brother Lélé's signal, Aïda's mother, with the remnants of a frail, dolorous, profound voice and a hand on her watchful daughter's shoulder, launched herself into a secular song, accompanied by her contemporary, Cousine Palo. With two voices, they wove beauty into the air.

Everybody was gathered along the bank of the headwaters. The women performed the libation, pouring water into water, clairin into water, white sand into water, black sand into water.

The officiants' voices could not reach the entire crowd, who lined up downstream, but they knew that something powerful and essential was taking place. They imagined lyrics and songs more beautiful than reality could ever produce. Ludovic was there. Commère Sophia, the elderly Résia, Gibril Cador, Franckel Bontemps, Moïse Placide, Sèvila Maîtresse-Caye, Désirée Possible, Gibril and Désirée's children, other women, other children, fathers and sons. Bérénice Jean-Baptiste standing, her dress fluttering in the wind, her face full of emotion, tearful, trembling to the roots of her reason. The men who, during the prayer, went to dig new branches for the river, the women who cleared a path in the mud to allow the procession to pass, hard at work in the sprinkling rain, were also there, in awe. It is worth noting that out of this mass of persevering, spiritual peasants rose a discrete form of trance—another name for that which we call community. Agonan did not pull out his banjo. Nor were there any drums or bugles. Only in moments like these—when a song rises from beneath the eager eyes, before everyone banded together against a recalcitrant river, when a spellbinding performance conveys beauty and mystery, supplication and commandment, rhythm and narration, inutility and efficacy—do we recognize, without uttering a word, the precise meaning of that powerful title: chantrèl queen. A renn chantrèl.

11

After the soggy setbacks, the plain was experiencing a kind of personal sadness. A dour indifference soon unravelled at the first signs of relief, while its inhabitants waited, asking themselves what still lay ahead. The peasants who were passing through began to make their way back home, subdued, as though the foul weather's only purpose had been to bring everyone together for the procession and the prayer. Pépé the Tempest set out on the road to Croix-des-Bouquets, believing that the deluge too, had gone—taking with it the trials and tribulations of her niece and cousin. Aïda and her mother, on the other hand, returned home without any trouble. It took them two days to settle in, the time each needed to return to their old habits: Aïda to silence, and her mother to her suffering. Nobody, in any story, should die without being explicitly given a name. Aïda's mother was named Gracilia France Placide.

The third night after returning home, at the moment just before sunrise when the little girl usually brought her mother water and a basin, she found her spread out like an object. Her face swollen, Gracilia had clearly failed to cough out her nocturnal pain this time. Aïda found her stiff and blue all over, nearly shimmering in the low light of the coming day. She soon realized that this meant death. She had never heard that corpses glimmered blue in the waking dawn.

Gracilia was dead. Aïda looked upon her, detached from herself by a feeling of desolation. She no longer felt the bottoms of her feet on the cold ground, and the walls of the room vibrated like a sound echoing in the distance. She had already poured out her soul in the past days, as her mother's illness worsened. Now that her mother's life force appeared to have left her for ever, Aïda felt something else. It was hard to say whether it was more intense. It was different. Up until this point, everything had been given to her first by her mother. Seeing her lying there, with the sheet covering her chest as though she had planned her departure, Aïda was completely overwhelmed, far removed from the world she had always known. The child sat for a moment at the foot of the bed, trembling for a long while, confronting the fact of her mother's death alone, without knowing the mournful cries of weeping commères from the Cul-de-Sac plain. A pincer grabbed and squeezed her heart. A prickly bubble swelled in her throat. The room emptied of all of its fresh morning air.

Aïda took a few moments to gather herself, then stepped out and walked on and on to tell the one most concerned that her mother had suddenly turned blue as daylight rose. Stiff.

*

Upon entering the front yard, Aïda noticed Ludovic Possible sitting on the verandah. Ludovic wished to rebuild this space, ravaged by the rain, to reclaim his posture, one hand on his shoulder, granting him the spitting image of a true leader who did not know it. He saw Aïda crossing the yard and felt the chair vanish beneath him. For more than five years, since he lost his wife and came to live here, he hoped and doubted, at once, that this moment would come.

Aïda approached and stared blankly at him, troubled and incapable of crying. The sun was already there, imposing its silvery presence. Ludovic went inside to look for a chair. He returned with a smaller chair and placed it next to his own. Aïda knew, instinctively, that sitting still was not the proper thing to do. So, she paced back and forth. Ludovic's house was identical to the ones owned by the former plantation owners. She was surrounded by equally divided parcels of land, with the verandah bordering two-thirds of them, such that one could turn around and see in every direction. This also meant that, apart from the vagaries of the cacti growing on the verge, one could spot a person turning round in every direction. Aïda was turning round, in every direction.

In the beginning, it was a slow and painful walk, as though she were trying to untangle something in her mind. She quickened her pace, although no less painful to watch, and the trail of the little girl grew longer, as though in penitence. She trudged around the house in one direction, then the other. She marched on, and her body, it seemed to Ludovic, reflected a combination of questioning and suffering—a sort of accusation. She was not asking what things were, but why they were, and had always been, that way. Ludovic sank into his chair made of woven cane. He collapsed, imploding. He watched distress unfold before him and understood his role. As an old man, he knew what to do and when to let out his tears. But he also knew that one's throat could become knotted, parched, and one's eyes could redden without allowing a single tear to escape.

*

About fourteen years ago, Ludovic still had a lady of the house—children and grandchildren who preserved his honour. From their main residence in Croix-des-Bouquets, the Possibles possessed the majority of arable land throughout the Cul-de-Sac plain and controlled the cost of labour. They bought from the smallest farms in the area, processed the foodstuffs and resold them. With a hand in every phase of production, they were, in a way, in competition with themselves—engaged in a subtle game where, without necessarily becoming the wealthiest family, they, along with their military allies, began to influence the laws governing wealth and poverty. In the era of strict Catholicism, Ludovic swore by God, Family and Country, just as his father had before him. He went out to his lands to secure his profits and observe the proper moral order of things when, in a breach of his best judgement, he planted in Gracilia a seed that would grow into little Aïda. There would not have been anything scandalous about it if he had declared: 'Attention, everyone! This young, penniless negro right here is pregnant by me; her child will be mine, and she is going to stay right here as my official concubine, just as she has been for years.' Nobody, not even Ludovic's wife, would have had any objections to it, as long as Gracilia remained in her simple role as the child's mother. What is more, without being accused of contradiction, Ludovic could have continued down the mulatto path, the heirs of the whites, upholding morality, God, Country and Property, by denouncing far and wide the scourge of polygamy. Instead, Ludovic chose the peace of mind of only having to deal with his marital household. He conceded a few parcels of land to Gracilia to grow tobacco, hoping to paint over his adulterous paternity with silence. The young Gracilia, for her part, never said a word to anyone. She was pregnant by grace of the Holy Spirit and hid herself away out of shame, giving up hope that one day Ludovic would leave his mulatress wife and city life to shack up with a peasant woman without a name.

*

As Ludovic settled down in Boën after the death of his wife, he did not seize the occasion to live out his unrealized domestic life with Gracilia. Quite the contrary, facing the facts that it was too late for them, a quiet timidity grew between them. Ludovic and Gracilia ultimately never spoke to each other again. Nor did anyone else ever share either of their beds. The absurd fidelity they forged out of failure seemed to make them happy, or they patiently tolerated it, until the past came knocking once more, right in front of Papa Possible, on this tense morning, as he watched Aïda continue to pace up and down.

Ludovic grimaced, stood up, and faced the little girl who had become his daughter for the first time. Aïda hardly flinched, uncertain of how to free herself from the cold grip of reality. The old man brought her inside. On the table, a cold, bitter, strong coffee awaited them. Neither of them had a sip. They sat around the table—Ludovic trying not to stare at Aïda, Aïda trying to unglue her eyes from the floor—both overwhelmed by this encounter, which felt like the first time they had seen each other, even though they were once accustomed to looking each other in the eye. They forgot all about poor Gracilia, whose remains awaited, lying on her back without an honourable hand to draw the white sheet over her face—a universal *sine qua non* for the passage from life to death.

*

Where did they find the strength—where did they get the nerve—to walk side by side like they did, without a word or a glance between them? One discovering, the other enduring anew, the cadaver that would lie between the two from this day onwards, potentially binding them together forever. Ludovic and Aïda were on their way to the girl's house, following each other's steps and feeding the silence of their distress. Ludovic was at the age of restraint, while Aïda had a deeply rooted, almost innate manner of not inserting useless words into the flow of events.

They reached Gracilia's verandah. The door was open. Aïda remained outside, looking out at the yard in front of her. Ludovic stepped inside. His body felt no sense of hesitation, but the rest of him, his spirit, recoiled at the sight of Gracilia France Placide's face: dark-blue, almost blue-black. A faint shimmer at the roots of her hair gave the impression of a halo. That was no way for anyone to die, Ludovic knew it. Yet there she was before him: the inert body of the woman who could have been—who should have become—his own, at least partly; whatever it would have taken to spare her from eternal shame, which is as blue as the sea, and as unfathomably deep.

*

Ludovic set out to find help, making sure that Aïda wouldn't see the body again—now covered from head to toe, the universal *sine qua non* for the passage from life, etc., etc. as mentioned earlier, not so long ago.

Papa Possible traversed the fields. Each time he placed his walking stick in front of him, followed by one foot after the other, he saw something from his past. These were not personal memories so much as echoes of the whole of Cul-de-Sac plain that resonated within him—the weight of history and geography. It was all a burden: death, Aïda, the army, the row of sugarcane he cut through, Gracilia whom he had not wed, the stories, his deceased wife. Ludovic recalled, as he traversed the fields, that he had not thought of his wife in a long time. He looked at the sugarcane plantation beside him, then at the one across the path. Sugarcane is finished, he thought. Ludovic, supported by his walking stick, carried on: one foot, then the other.

Sugarcane is finished. Those with long memories—who remember when one thousand seven hundred plots of land were covered with sugary stalks, worked vigorously, feverishly by shackled hands—will tell you with defiance, satisfaction, regret or passion that sugar cane is finished. The parcels of land dedicated to the cultivation of sugarcane are a pale reflection of a legend that goes way back. The plain of Cul-de-Sac is not what she used to be. Once, the Baron Étienne Louis Ferron de

La Ferronnays forged in his name a domain so extensive, a plantation so vast, that he could not cross it in a single day. Dissatisfied by his present situation, Étienne Louis entered into a marriage contract with Marquise Marie Élisabeth Timothée Binau, an extremely wealthy Creole woman from Grande Rivière in the northern plain. A fatal error on the part of the baron, since the marquise, besides her more-than-comfortable lineage and dowry, harboured two other, more discrete, nearly imperceptible talents: her adoration of carnal relations and her hatred of opportunists.

To this day, the entire plain knows the story, Ludovic reckons, they all know how after having amassed so much wealth, after having led the colony of Saint Domingue as deputy governor, then interim governor, the Baron de La Ferronnays returned to his native Brittany to live the sad life of an absentee colonist, leaving his dishonourable wife to the mosquitoes. Without delay, our marquise began multiplying her adventures, lovers and beautiful amorous liaisons, with a clear preference for sable skin: free Black people, freed men and women, or the progeny of whites and negroes, mulattoes. Creole negroes born in the colony, or bosals freshly arrived from Africa. Everyone passed through. She populated the country with little *sang-mêlés,* mixed-blood children, and distributed so much of her lands that the baron took matters into his own hands. In order to save the latifundia system, that is, the plantation-like scheme of land ownership, the stupendous monoculture of sugarcane, and to reify his racial pride, he had his own wife captured and forcibly deported to the French metropole, then left her for dead, immured in a convent. Baron Ferron de La Ferronnays conceded the remaining lands to a member of his family. But since History, with a capital H, does not have a reverse gear, the latifundia and monoculture did not survive the revolt of the Black, enslaved people of Saint Domingue, the dispossession of the white colonists, absentee or assiduous, or the new social and ethnic configuration with whites no longer atop the pyramid, leaving vacancies for Affranchis, Black people and mulattoes. This is the story of the newest fracture between the urban and the rural, between island-born creoles and bosals, since, as we have previously established, sugarcane is finished. At this point, Ludovic realized that he had already arrived at Brother Lélé's.

From here, the adults work together to determine the next steps. The urgency mounts. Everything needs to be done for tomorrow's wake, my friends! Decomposition pays no mind to a renn chantrèl, a singing queen. We bury her the day after tomorrow, and everything will appear as though we are caught in an unusual routine. We are repeating the same gestures under completely different circumstances.

This is what death is: a popular festivity for the countryside where we observe the peasants exorcising the departed with dances, debauchery, storytelling, copious food and lubricious wisecracks in equal measure. Ludovic took charge of everything, hoping to make amends for the life he had not given to Gracilia and their daughter. In the evening, he would set about the reconstruction of his tomb. Though they had not lived together, there would always be a place for Aïda's mother by his side on the eternal voyage, when they would assuredly follow the same routine of fidelity and abstinence. The news of Gracilia's funeral spread across the plain as quickly as the wind. The morning after her death, cows, pigs and goats were already en route to the abattoir.

Cups filled with clairin, mournful commères cleansed the garb of their final apparition in the sun, while the men gossiped about the fate of the deceased's possessions.

*

It just so happens that, in this case, the property of the deceased person is not clear to anyone. Had she possessed nothing to bequeath, the matter would be much simpler. In his function as notary, Ludovic Possible would have written: 'without inheritance or succession'—and everyone would have known that one of the many wretched of the earth had resided here. But Aïda's mother left behind a legacy: plots of tobacco across numerous plantations. She left behind a deliberate and reserved way of walking life's path, almost as though apologizing for having trod upon the soil. She passed that outlook on life to Aïda, her silent daughter. Gracilia also left behind a new bond of kinship, for Aïda had suddenly become Papa Possible's daughter, aware of what a man might do when he has more than a decade of amends to make.

Ludovic paid for the victuals at the wake, as well as for all the burial preparations. He also spread the word that this funeral, unlike the others, would be grandiose. Because he, Ludovic Possible, decided that such a chantrèl—majestic and generous with her voice—should not depart just like that, with everyone's indifference. He made the decisions and the peasants did the work. It was not so much that they were intrigued by the profound sentiments guiding Papa Possible—whether they spoke to his contradictions or to his redemption—but, rather, that this death had come at a timely moment for public celebration. Boën, Vaudreuil, La Mardelle, Peyrac, Juan, all the way to Thomazeau and Ganthier, every neighbouring village had endured the whims of the weather. The peasants had just been cooped up on their farms for two weeks, all dreaming of bloody roosters killing one another. Somewhere among them, lost in the background, lingered Balthazar Possible's threats of reprisals. There were unresolved debts following the betting in the cockfighting ring. There were tombs to rebuild, houses to raise again, lost garden plots, mud, filth, the beginnings of dust—so many things to purge that everyone deserved a festivity as dolorous as death. If the death of a woman airs a family's dirty laundry, then it is there for the taking—everything is there for the taking. A woman who, in parting, left the plain with as many stories still to unfold as she had told in her life—once upon a time.

12

Alcohol flowed like water at the wake, changing the colour of things. Game tables of cards and dominoes, tiny factions of wheelers, dealers and braggarts—everything teemed with excitement when, suddenly, Big-Bellied Dorilien decided to unload one of his seven hundred seventy-seven sacks of stories. Among the griots, rambling songsmiths and cocky storytellers of all types that wandered the earth, Big-Bellied Dorilien was the most characteristic, the most renowned, the most reviled and somehow the most venerated of the Cul-de-Sac plain. His reputation preceded him by one hundred paces, and everyone knew that for a wake—whether you liked it or not, for better or worse—it was best to count Big-Bellied Dorilien among your ranks than the other way around. He was the essential presence at every bamboche worth its salt; thanks to that, Big-Bellied Dorilien lived large, eating and drinking his fill without having to plant anything besides bawdy, befuddling tales. *Krik? Krak! Èske lakou a dòmi? No, the lakou is not asleep! Oh, well, if the yard is not asleep, allow me to tell you how this did that and how here is there and there is here!* In short, Big-Bellied Dorilien was a trickster, a prestidigitator of words, a merry man of happy people. Papa Possible avoided this big-bellied blabbermouth as much as he could—someone who observed no taboos and demanded payment for his mere presence, making it just as possible for him to choose to keep his beak shut as to steal the words from everyone else's mouth, depending on the whims of his state of inebriation. In fact, he was the only one who had ever dared to crack a joke about the mute, fatherless girl and her virgin mother in a corner of Boën, knocked up by the Holy Spirit or God Our Father himself, who knows, and, ever since, he had never been invited back to play in the cockfighting arena. But for this evening alone, Ludovic wanted it all. He consented to receiving Big-Bellied Dorilien, and impatiently waited for him to speak.

Dorilien made an outrageous display of himself. He came across as a person of refinement and boorishness in the same breath and movement. He wore an African boubou with elegance, an item of clothing known as an *agbádá*, a daring move in these days when the less one wore a frock coat and waistcoats, the further one is considered to be from the human race. He arrived and shook his impressive story-filled belly by stomping the ground, sometimes emitting the same sound from his mouth—*boom, boom, boom*—for each stamp of his foot. Then his voice rose: 'In this belly I have here,' he thundered, 'there are no fewer than seven hundred and seventy-seven sacks of stories, and of these, I have yet to unload even a quarter of a single one!'

'*Èske lakou a dòmi?,*' he asked, as usual, to call people's attention before beginning a story.

'No, the *lakou* is not asleep!,' the villagers replied.

And so, the worthy sire began his tale.

Naturally, he knew just about everything there was to know. If he didn't, he made it up on the spot while staring into your soul. Every story, told in a certain way, exudes a true rhythm. You breathe in, so to speak, all the narrative threads he weaves together. Better still, you want to know more. For example, why is the sky so far from the earth, if not because at the dawn of time old lady Dédé, outraged by God the Father, beat the earth with the handle of her pestle? Since then, the Most High has exiled his kingdom and paid no mind to the problems down below. Why are donkeys donkeys, and horses horses? How did the sea become blue, and the blood of all humanity red? Dorilien extrudes answers for you from his big belly, and you believe them with all that remains of the child within you.

He was also well known for Bouki the Baffled and Malice the Cunning—characters he handled better than anyone else. And for good reason! He was not far from having invented them himself, since before him, nobody had ever heard of Bouki and Malice.

Yet, special occasions call for special tales, so on this evening, Dorilien set himself apart from the *lodyanseurs*—the bumptious band of cheap storytellers gathered at the back of the school (or what was left of it after the foul weather). He was more connected, shared a closer tie with this family. He felt all the tensions resurrected by this dead body, and he acknowledged little Aïda's pain in having to live without her mother from here on. He also preferred not to provoke Papa Possible any further on the subject of hidden filiation. He was eccentric, but he had not lost his mind, and one could sense a fine line—an imaginary boundary between provocation and indecency—that he had never quite crossed, despite everything.

*

The ramblers and their acolytes competed for the most salacious language. In other words, the wake was beginning to heat up—as any good gathering of this kind should. Right then and there, Dorilien pounded the earth three times with his left foot, causing his entire bodily mass to shake.

'*Èske lakou a dòmi?*'

'No, the yard is not asleep!'

If the *lakou* is not asleep, it should know that death is not always the path for everyone. Long, long ago, in a time before time existed, those who created things did not die. After experiencing old age or illness, at the moment when death arrived, everyone who had created something—singers, dancers, architects, masons, farmers, healers, scientists, the irrational, dogs, cats, rascals and the gods—all the women and men who had ever invented something, who had changed the course of shared knowledge, or who had made something out of nothing, would receive a notice granting life for as long as their creation existed. Dorilien recounted how creation came to be, and how the creators, content with what they had made, were born again in the land of their inventions. As time went on, someone eventually invented hatred; then another person came up with jealousy; this one conceived slavish imitation; and that one, limitless anger. Not all creations are necessarily good, and throughout history disagreements emerged—conflicts between masons and farmers, the irrational and the gods, cats and dogs. Brer Dog and Brer Cat no longer agree on anything. One has no shame, while the other has no respect for anyone else. Who the hell invented private property, so that no sort of creation can be possible without a dispute, without a tension between what one earns and what one brings to the table. And so Big-Bellied Dorilien's stories go. One never knows how he causes us to laugh or reflect so much. It depends. But we always want to know what will happen next.

Dorilien dug up two or three new little tales. A small crowd gathered around him, without overshadowing the entire wake. Paloma Placide, our Pépé the Tempest, ensured that the evening unfolded as planned, that everyone remained in line, glimmering amid the most perfect chaos.

*

Pépé was at home in Croix-des-Bouquets when Balthazar Possible brought her the news of Gracilia's death.

Balthazar had known and respected Paloma for ages. They were allies and had always agreed to protect Boën from the agrarian system run by the army. When the commercial deficit was conceived under the weight of the independence debt, along with the negotiations to lessen the payments, the government of our ever-devoted Jean-Pierre Boyer set about enforcing the rural code with great severity. The peasants could not—and still cannot—sell their produce in the city without going through the military authorities, who impose levies at will. The bourgeois are prohibited from directly selling the produce harvested on their lands because one must not enrich a few Black peasants in the process. Except that Balthazar and Pépé the Tempest contravene this territorial embargo as best as they can. Balthazar ensures that Pépé leaves goods, tools, textiles and all manner of processed products to be harvested and sold by farmers on site. Meanwhile, Paloma Placide whispers in the ears of the potentates, the decorated members of the government and the military, guaranteeing that Balthazar can play the roles of agrarian deputy, rural police officer, section chief and commune commandant without the inconvenience of a uniform or paying too close attention to legality.

Balthazar was already emotional when he arrived at Paloma's and stood at the threshold, at the entrance to her little garden in the yard.

'There are two pieces of bad news,' he started to say, 'and we have to talk about them.'

Dressed in a large blue apron, Paloma put aside her watering can, went inside to her front room—with its sparse furnishings and high ceilings—offered her guest a chair, and sat down to learn that Aïda's mother had died. In the flicker of an eyelid, Paloma Placide was overcome, numb, when Balthazar added, as though to finish her off: 'There's also this—I no longer want to cover for anyone in the plain. No more negotiations or financial schemes. Illicit business no longer has a place here. All for one, and shit for all.'

Paloma has been aware of the mounting tensions between Balthazar and everyone else since the killing of his proud cock, the Vile Beast. She had been anticipating a decision rooted in anger. In seeking to breach their collaboration, however, Balthazar revealed something more: a confused feeling of nostalgia for a faraway land that never existed. Forgetting her own grief at once, Paloma attributed Balthazar's reaction to a new level of cruelty, one born out of a nameless sadness, a profound sense of regret. Balthazar had come to realize that a world in which Gracilia could perish without ever having been properly loved or cherished was, in fact, as cruel as it seemed.

Balthazar's emotional state was laid out on the table in front of them, to be scrutinized like a piece of money. Paloma Placide did not wish to delve into the details. This time, that was it. Things were serious. The man before her had grown old; wrinkles had formed on his brow, and there was something mysterious, almost divine, in his features. He was no longer the quadroon of yesteryear, the cruel dandy who took pleasure in quarrelling with his older brother. He was a lonely man—sad, remorseful and devastated.

*

'What are you planning to do?' she asked, not without a trace of bitterness.

After that question, everyone would have to choose a side. Paloma had already chosen to support Ludovic Possible and protect Aïda because, after thirteen years of waiting, the opportunity had come for her to feel like a mama—an aching mama, the one-and-only mother who would give endless love, in turn, reap the satisfaction of seeing a happy daughter, of watching her grow up, and saying to herself: that's me.

'I'm going to see Commandant Saurel,' Balthazar replied. 'I'm going to claim the titles of rural officer and section chief. I'll make Boën a military district—double the size, if possible, of a parish. You, me, all mulattos in power, all the way to the President of the Republic, we are all threatened by these factious people who call themselves revolutionaries. Disorder has gone on for far too long . . . it is time to fall in line.'

In saying all this, Balthazar held tight to the reins of his sang-froid. He breathed heavily between each sentence, a telltale sign that he was making a considerable effort to contain himself, which he managed. This allowed Paloma and him to share a grey, twisted silence, during which she finished contemplating the contours of her emotional state.

'You could have done something, too.' Pépé the Tempest said, raising her bet. 'You and your brother, with your ridiculous little cockfights, you left her to die in her corner, alone with her daughter, full of shame and misery. You could have done something, too.'

These words were a pain in Balthazar's neck, ears, his palate, and then his throat. He took his time, aware that Paloma could not truly be angry with him. He closed his eyes for a few moments, reopened them, breathed deeply, then said, in a suddenly hoarse voice:

'It is that bastard Ludovic. Everything belongs to him—everything has always belonged to him. What do you know about Gracilia France, about her hopes, about her despair? It's not because you share the same patronym, like one baptises their property, like one baptises their lands, their personal property, *biens meubles*. It's not because you called her *cousine* . . . It's that bastard Ludovic!'

Balthazar managed to catch his breath.

'We have mistreated these people. We have dispossessed them, spoiled them, raised them in ignorance, deliberately and by force. We have abused these people . . . '

And with the last of his breath, he said:

'They are going to avenge themselves. I'll still be here to protect your rosy ass, but they will seek revenge.'

As he left, Balthazar flung these words at his hostess, 'Paloma, I know you to be a courageous woman. My only hope is that you will not stand in my way when I strike against that filthy Timoléon and that bastard Ludovic.'

'You know very well that I'll be standing in your way, and I shall kill you, if the time comes.'

'Here we are, two lost men.'

'I am a woman.'

'Just as I thought.'

And so, Cousine Palo found herself in the corner, chiding over here, consoling and reassuring over there. She knew that Timoléon Jean-Baptiste, who mostly kept to himself, needed to know that he was not alone, and Ludovic needed to know that he was not so judged, and everyone else needed to know that Paloma Placide, also known as Pépé the Tempest, *fanm djanm*, had not had her final say on what should and should not be.

*

As for Aïda, she was rather calm given the occasion. Rather surprised that so many people had come to see her dead mother whom, apart from the mention of certain people, real and imaginary, Aïda had always considered lonely. The *lakou* teemed with people eating and cursing into the night, unconcerned with how the poor woman was holding up, lying on her back in her place of truth. Aïda would not be allowed to see her mother's body again until tomorrow afternoon at the burial. All she could do was secretly wonder how she was feeling at the time: what would happen to her after death, or whether all of this might turn out to be an immense farce, a rite of passage from childhood to adulthood? One never knows. Aïda wondered whether Ludovic would regain his composure and explain to her everything that had happened in the last couple of hours. She was completely lost in thought by the end of Dorilien's final story, as he awaited applause and praise.

And at that very moment, Aïda stood up without hesitation or haste. She faced the crowd, cutting short the ovations, and began telling her own story.

Aïda spoke with a certain assurance. She improvised a little nursery rhyme to go along with her story—both very simple and pure—in front of the most skilled orator of the Cul-de-Sac plain. Aïda, a girl of almost thirteen years, cloaked in sadness, who, most of the time, hardly ever spoke. People took her for a simpleton, a fool, a shadow hunter. Clothed in the same little blue caraco she had worn when she foretold the death of the serviceman Pierre Saurel, she was now improvising, just like that, in front of everyone. She rattled off a nursery rhyme and a story laced with poetry.

It was the well-known story of the old woman carrying her cord of firewood on her head as her penance. The old woman walked and walked and walked, always straight ahead, never changing direction, despite numerous encounters. She walked and walked and walked, until she ended up on the moon. In fact, Aïda said, on nights when the moon is full, all you need to do is lift your head to see her still walking, following her lunar path with her little cord of firewood on her head as her penance.

While many knew this story, everyone felt that Aïda made something new of it. Perhaps because she punctuated the silences differently. Aïda does not tell; she shows you each and every detail. When the old woman meets the storm, Aïda shows you the force of the wind. When the old woman encounters the evil vipers, Aïda squirts venom in your face. Aïda alone speaks to you with the voice of the little cord of firewood that was the old woman's penance. She shows you how sad it was for the little cord of firewood to be the penance of the old woman who walked and walked and walked until she ended up on the moon's surface. But the cord of wood never had a choice; it had to remain the penance of the old woman who would, one day, complete her journey by laying her burden down on the swaying surface of the sun. *Èske lakou a dòmi?*

13

Aïda was living with Ludovic, who had once again become a stranger to her. She noticed certain inhabitants paying him a great deal of attention, showing him benevolence. Things began to rearrange themselves inside her young mind, like the rooms of a house. In recent days, she would wake in the middle of the night without ever leaving her bed. On Saturday night, a month after the burial, she received a visit from the rooster that previously haunted life on the plain of Cul-de-Sac, or perhaps from another.

Aïda went to lie down on her straw mattress, which lay empty, waiting for an adventurous child. She reminisced about the day while attempting to make out the ceiling in the darkness. The wooden frame, the tile roof, a tiny grey anole charting its course between the two. Everything was visible—the last stray fly looking out for itself, the spider that would eventually eat the fly, the path of termites nibbling on the wood, as well as a few nocturnal flying insects without names. At this age, it was unusual not to fill one's night with sleep, but that was how things had been since Gracilia's death. She would go to bed in the evening, fall asleep, then wake again. She awaited visitors the whole night, lying on this foreign bed. No door separated her from the rest of the house. Only a large grey curtain, or what was left of it, next to which shimmered a gentle cotton flame, devouring itself in oil: the night light.

Aïda saw a passing shadow. She heard what sounded like a cackling hen. Outside, the blackest night crushed the chirping of crickets. Only the song of the leaves clung to the mysteriousness of the passing time. It wasn't a gallinaceous time of day. Even so, Aïda noticed a second shadow and discovered a rooster approaching the foot of her bed. She did not startle. This time, the bird was the proper size. Far from the human-sized rooster she had heard people talking about almost everywhere. She was curious to find out what this creature was. Was it Biss the Undefeated? Was it the Vile Beast? Was it one of the many winged gladiators whose names had become legends? Aïda tried to sit up to solve the mystery. Impossible. She felt the weight of a man seated on her body, or perhaps her chest, growing so heavy that she couldn't lift herself. She gave in and watched the rooster approach, coming closer, strutting around her bed frame, clucking, watching her, and then leaving as swiftly as he had arrived.

Something happens when the sun comes up. The growing light, or the receding darkness, dilutes insomnia, amplifies nightmares and eases pain. Let's call it dawn. Dawn ushered Aïda into the day's embrace, and this rooster, at once so alive, was perhaps a dream. Aïda woke and felt as though she were a part of this world. She also received a message from the rooster: she was indeed one of them. The solidarity of her nightmare did not prevent her from becoming aware of another, even more radical, feeling of integration—Aïda could feel her blood flowing. As she sat up, she felt a slight warmth between her thighs. She looked at her white nightgown, stained with a diaphanous red. Aïda had become a woman.

*

To introduce her newfound self to Ludovic Possible, the young girl displayed her nightgown over a chair next to the dining table. This bold gesture was the only way she knew to apprise her new parent of the news. In fact, understanding very well what was happening to her, she immediately realized that Ludovic was the only person to whom she could entrust her intimacy. In this way, perhaps the old man had finally become someone important to her. Just then, he walked in by chance to drink his coffee. He saw the gown on the chair. 'That's it, it's begun,' he mumbled. A trace of panic lingered between his eyebrows, as though he had been expecting bad news that had arrived too soon.

The morning continued in a protracted freefall. Ludovic sat beside the table, cleared his throat, confronted his modesty, and then asked Aïda:

'Do you know how to take care of it?'

The young girl could hear perfectly and understood what he wished to say. She did not respond. Ludovic, lost at sea in a way he had rarely been during his life as a leader, added: 'I have no idea . . . what to do,' as though he was speaking to himself.

'We have to tell my Aunt Paloma.'

And so, Pépé the Tempest was officially inducted in Aïda's life as a maternal figure.

She would no longer be distant, making round trips to the plain and ensuring that Ludovic didn't become too lost in his role as a parent, a role he seemed to have forgotten over the years. Aïda dove into Paloma's reassuring embrace. When Pépé arrived at the house, Aïda stowed away the sadness she had been nurturing the entire day, and re-emerged from her corner to greet her aunt with a smile. Paloma warranted nothing less, certainly in terms of good humour. Covered in jewellery, this thunderous woman, magnificently plump, possessing ironclad self-assurance, always announced her presence by launching words, orders, or comments in front of her. One could be in the main room, the backyard, or in the kitchen, and hear, 'I am not planning to stand around! Quick, bring me a chair, and don't forget a cushion!' and know that Paloma had landed. Or sometimes, 'Oh, I'll just do it myself. Everyone in this house is useless,' and Paloma just solved your problem right where she stood. In some ways, one might wonder if things were better after Gracilia's death. That 'one' who could have been was most certainly not the little orphaned girl. Perhaps it was the crude language of the peasantry, which had nothing better to do than to report what the eyes saw. Because it was true, the question lingered: when a nearly vanishing woman was lost, but this grandiose, quick-witted tempest of a woman with a musical cadence and a dishevelled voice was gained, one cannot help but conclude that things have turned out for the best, if one analyses the situation objectively. The 'one' remains cruel, and Aïda, the concerned party, never considered whether she preferred this mother to her own.

Her Aunt Paloma, *cousine* in her deceased mother's heart, had always been larger than life. Aïda saw her more frequently now and no longer had Gracilia silently remind her that life was made up of shame and consolation, reticence and everyday battles. Nevertheless, Aïda was, in some ways, a consolation for Paloma Placide. Paloma adopted Aïda. Aïda embraced Paloma. They made a good match and shared a certain joy in the reunion. They talked about everything and nothing, accompanied each other in their daily tasks at Ludovic's house. They drew gaiety and tranquillity from each other, completing one another like teeth and gums.

*

Ludovic, in his own way, did what he could to be as available to Aïda as possible. But in reality, it was the opposite, because as the days passed, little by little, the girl's primary concern became looking after her fragile companion. In the morning, she woke up and went to the kitchen behind the house, where the wood was already prepared for a fire—something she had thought about the night before. She lit the fire and made the coffee. If the bread wasn't fresh enough, she would go out before daybreak, if necessary, and bring back warm bread. When Ludovic lingered in bed, unable to get up on his own, Aïda would hold his hand and tell him that the sun was likely to show up on the verandah before him, which he did not appreciate. Soon Papa Possible would make an effort, dragging himself with Aïda's help all the way to his washbasin. When he could count on nobody, Ludovic had completely forgotten his age and the fatigue that came with being a respectable man. He did everything alone and efficiently. Now that Aïda was sleeping in the room next door, old age settled in, and, sometimes, despite his initial discomfort, Ludovic would accept help even with his bath.

Aïda scrubbed Ludovic's back. His arms and underarms, too. She slowed a little on his chest, then moved lower. His stomach, his groin, his thighs. Ludovic stopped her. He still wanted to wash his feet and his intimate parts himself. He was still able to. But mostly, he could not stand the sight of it. He did not believe he deserved to see this young lady in the prime of her life, whom he had only just accepted as his own child and had scorned for so long, in such a predicament. He couldn't stand the idea of her squatting down in front of him, washing his feet with her two hands. Aïda could tell. One day, he would not be able to, and she would have to do it. In the meantime, the coffee grew cold again. She went to warm it up. She pulled out the large straw chair, set the table outside, and placed the walking stick on the verandah in case Ludovic decided to go for a stroll.

The patriarch's fatigue, which had begun with the recent deluge and was worsened by Gracilia's funereal proceedings, did not favour the effort to get Boën and its surroundings back on their feet. The ruins of the cockfighting ring no longer boasted any pride. A few tombs remained cracked down to the base. As for the schoolhouse, it was a reminder of nothing more than crude mistakes. A few children stopped by, including Jean-Zamor and his brother Doréus, but they appeared to be visiting Aïda more than attending school. The structure had lost a third of its palm-frond roof, which did not seem to bother anyone. During the unexpected downpours in March, the benches were drenched by the full force of the rain. The dirt floor bore holes that resembled little ponds, bothersome before Gracilia's wake, and since then filled with white sand. The sun of the first days of May had begun to assert itself. Everything turned to dust and potholes, calling forth the despair of a plain growing heavier, preparing itself for harsh heat.

Bérénice Jean-Baptiste made a sincere attempt to restore the normal routine for teaching the children. She showed up every morning with a rake, a shovel and a broom, but the students' persistent absenteeism thwarted her best efforts. She told herself that things were probably better this way, a momentary pause would allow the space to flourish once more. Perhaps next autumn, she would turn it into something that more closely resembled a properly accredited institution, like those in the cities far from the plain of Cul-de-Sac.

*

Something else, something intangible, was also beginning to take shape in this world that was coming undone—the young Aïda's growing reputation as a chantrèl. After hearing the story of the little cord of wood, after admiring the way the girl layered the words onto the canvas of her characteristic silence, Big-Bellied Dorilien never ran out of panegyrics to describe the moment. Throughout his travels as a performer, he spoke backstage of the beguiling charm of a storytelling child who was otherwise nearly mute, yet whose every word made you vibrate with its every element and presence.

One week after the wake, Dorilien was in Croix-des-Bouquets in the company of the old district commandant, Éric Saurel, to celebrate the annual festivities. The nobles had gathered in preparation for the proposed World Fair, which had been scheduled and postponed every year for at least a decade. Dorilien was simply one of their own. He was comfortable, drinking and laughing. In short, he was happy, doing what he did best: mingling with the jubilant crowd and roaring louder than the rest. On the way out, face to face with Éric Saurel, he remarked:

'It's crude to make people laugh like that.'

'What would you prefer? To make them cry?'

'No. To move them, like Aïda, the little girl in Boën.'

Since then, he began referring to Aïda in his own stories, making her into a mysterious character—a great weaver of words. Among his seven hundred seventy-seven sacks of stories, spread out throughout the country from north to south, east to west, there are several that speak of embellishers, illusionists, charmers and healers. There were so many that it was not difficult, and the circumstances almost seemed to call for him to shower Aïda with these magical roles. Instead of some unknown tamer whispering messages of tenderness into the ears of wild animals, it was a young girl from the plain who possessed this miraculous gift. Instead of an unknown healing wordsmith, it was a child from Boën revealing her therapeutic powers. Instead of some hypnotist manipulating the beauty of silence, it was a young girl from the plain who wielded this magnetic gift. He took a step further to the point of claiming that impotent men were visiting Aïda by the dozens, not far from the White River, just as he spoke, so that she could pronounce a few words about their virility and instantly restore their Spartan vigour.

Maybe this was the boundary that should not have been crossed, since when it came to healing, especially for such essential matters, nobody could tell the difference between the farcical legends of a jester and the modest life of a songstress. As the weeks passed, still without having had the chance to make a single public appearance after her mother's wake, Aïda's reputation had already reached a point where it demanded her to break her silence to be consecrated once and for all.

*

Truth be told, Aïda continued to consume stories and recount them. She was not like Dorilien, who was always thirsting for a stage to practise his art. She learnt the art of the word in the most discreet intimacy, it was her mother tongue in the truest sense, passed down through what her mother had shared with her. It was like following in Gracilia France Placide's footsteps while singing a song to the White River as she did the washing. Talking with Jean-Zamor on the verandah at night, telling him of lands where no one from the plain had ever been, was like embracing her mother. So too was recounting the tale of the discord between cats and dogs to Ti Beau, the spaniel, who only listened with one ear.

Soon, three months had passed since she lost her mother. Though its waters were low, the river continued to flow, indifferent to the nostalgia of the river rocks. The inhabitants felt as if their daily lives flashed before their eyes, ever since the foul weather had left them unsettled. It wasn't as though they had stopped doing the same things—on Thursday nights, rounds of dominoes unfolded in the same silence on Ludovic's verandah. Timoléon Jean-Baptiste could be found there, no longer threatening anyone or provoking duels, placing his dominoes while awaiting the fate he knew was coming soon. Bérénice Jean-Baptiste could be seen there, providing order and a sliver of sense to the lives of the others. Agonan played his banjo. Brother Lèlè said his prayers. Mama Résia prepared her medicinal herbs before new maladies even called for them. Cockfighting no longer took place in Boën, but it carried on successfully in La Mardelle or Vaudreuil, sometimes even as far as Ganthier. No, their habits hadn't really changed. It was just that the inhabitants shared a sense of having missed the stagecoach, of having skipped a hut, as if they were waiting for something. Ever since they started dreaming of giant roosters, ever since the weather had unleashed itself in March instead of May, and their eternal protector and tyrant, Balthazar Possible, seemed to be seeking a divorce and promising nothing but their ruin, they felt as though something was coming.

14

In the twists and turns of the circumstances, Aïda reclaimed her material heritage—the tobacco business.

After Gracilia's burial, no one had set foot in their humble abode in the bowels of Boën. When Aïda ventured alone there for the first time, the journey from Papa Possible's to her former home seemed to pass quickly. It was a path of rediscovery, and, resigned to crossing the threshold into adult survival, she slipped into the skin of her new self.

A sliver of the sun settled on the porch just as Aïda opened the door. The light flooded the main room. She paid no attention to the bed and the sheets where she had last seen her mother. With quiet resolve, she walked towards the cabinet where a few jars of flavoured tobacco were kept. She took several jars, unravelled bunches and bunches of vines, opened sacks of dried tobacco, spread them out on the table, sorted through them, gathered what she needed, and left. She made her way to the production house a few paces away in the yard. Aïda could not recall ever having entered the building without her mother. Also, combined with the aroma of the already dried tobacco hanging in front of her, the memory of her mother reached her nose, a smell that she would never ever be without, for as long as she continued to steep her life in the exhalation of dried leaves. Aïda rolled her first-ever joint. She had already brought it to her lips when she realized that, to smoke, one must produce a flame, something rather onerous, given the iron and flint required to summon that subtle element, indispensable for everything from a spark to a blaze. So there she was, compelled to honour her dead mother by ingesting a dose of powdered tobacco through the back of her nose, instead of smoking it with the pride of the gesture. Aïda maintained this modest custom for the rest of her life, never once coughing after swallowing, so as not to lose face in her own presence.

On the day after the visit to her mother's house, Aïda set out on her first outing as a merchant. She decided not to sell at the markets like before, but to go door-to-door to fill up her days. Rather than carry a small basket on her head, Aïda persuaded Désirée, the neighbour, with the offer of three shiny new gourdes, to let her saddle up a donkey. Together, they chose the scrawny little black one named Satan, which they loaded with dried leaves, jars, vines and leather satchels full of tobacco.

Aïda was on her way. The journey beginning in Boën would take her across the entire eastern side of the plain. She would stop by O'Gorman, passing by everyone, then to Juan, mauled by yaws, all the way to Bojeu, where the earth is blue, to ultimately wind up at the small village of Ganthier, before turning around. Along the way, the inhabitants greeted Aïda with a chair and a snack—coffee, tea, sugar and biscuits—or quite simply with blessed fresh water to drink, as they waited for her to say what she had to say, as though what mattered most was not buying or selling, but meeting like old friends. Aïda went from one chair to another the whole blessed day, uncertain of what people wanted from her, unable to see how speaking to these strangers would benefit her business. She returned from her first day without having sold a single gram. And so, she discovered the hollow charm of commerce, where, after walking and tiring out her legs, all she gained was an evening's rest, which was only necessary for walking and tiring her legs once more the next day, in the whirlwind of a new corvée. That was what that routine felt like, but without the official designation.

Two days later, Aïda decided to bring along Ti Beau, the spaniel, who could be of some help against enemies on the lonely, unmarked roads between the bayahonda shrubs and the rows of sugarcane fields. Ti Beau could also defend her from the discourteous dogs of certain unfriendly houses. After four days, Aïda found herself on the road not only with Satan and Ti Beau, but also with the two other dogs, Le Maître and Le Grand. It was a journey whose commercial potential held no promise, and each moment made known the acidic taste of disillusionment.

At the end of the fourth day, as the light of the day declined, effacing the lingering shades of hope, Aïda considered leaving the sale of tobacco behind. This might be the last house before she dedicated her life to something else. She found herself in Vaudreuil, hollering good evening and announcing merchandise for sale in front of the tiny fence that led to Big-Bellied Dorilien's home.

*

Among the things one might find hard to imagine about the plain of Cul-de-Sac, like anywhere else for that matter, was that Dorilien did not live in a grotto with all sorts of wild and fantastical animals, with sirens who spoke the language of bygone buccaneers, with the living dead who, having tasted salt, pranced about all the blessed day, with child sorcerers blind by day and sighted by night. Instead, he lived in a house with a yard, a garden, a foundation and a roof. The most unbelievable thing was that he had a wife and children. At home, he did other things besides laugh and spin legendary stories.

When Aïda passed through his gate deep in the afternoon that Tuesday, Dorilien roared with a silly grin, 'God in heaven, this looks like a story that will end poorly!' Then he told Aïda to sit down and explained what life had in store for her. Conscious of the effects of his propaganda and the sowing of his tall tales, Dorilien accepted his avarice and suggested that Aïda tell two or three wisecracks at each house she hoped to sell tobacco. 'You must show them the world,' he told her. 'We are the lone glimmer in the night of their monotonous lives. Tell them two or three insignificant things, and they will find a way to hand you their money, even if it's under the pretext of buying tobacco.'

This mercantile tactic seemed so crude to Aïda that she thought she would rather never set foot in another farmer's home again than lure them in with her flair for storytelling. After all, she was selling tobacco not out of necessity, but to fill her days without school or, perhaps more profoundly, to cherish Gracilia's memory. She had no need to plod through the dust like this, hoping to sell what had not belonged to her for so long.

When she expressed her intention to continue the tobacco business, Ludovic Possible, without contesting her decision, did nothing to encourage her. His respectful silence was that of a prudent man who sought to understand, not wanting to impose on a young life not yet ready for such burdens. Ludovic guaranteed a roof over Aïda's head and bread on the table, which was better and more than she could ever have hoped for. But Aïda wanted to make something of her past; she wished to continue being her mother's daughter—she wished to exist. She took up the tobacco business, hitting the road with her donkey and her dogs until she found herself in Vaudreuil, standing before the impertinent Dorilien, who asked her to play the fool like a dishonourable wayfarer. She pictured the scenario of bewitchment proposed by her host and kept her disagreement to herself.

Dorilien accompanied Aïda into his yard, all the way to the gate, and placed a heavy hand on her back. This paternal gesture, as though an act of baptism, unsettled the young girl, who had had so little contact with this portly man. Dorilien, himself, mustered a certain courage and, just as he was about to bid Aïda farewell, showed her a notebook filled with papers folded onto themselves. He pulled out two of the sealed and stamped papers. On the back of each, clearly written in beautiful, ornate calligraphy, was the word 'Duels'. Then he said to Aïda, 'If you cross paths with Timoléon, I ask you to hand him this note on my behalf. And to Lorénel, you shall give the other.'

She could not help but pass by Timoléon's home, as he had become her closest neighbour, so to speak. As for Lorénel, he was a complete mystery—the man lived with a handful of sheep and few unique possessions in his yard in La Mardelle. He appeared in those parts wearing an old, tanned leather vest over his bare torso, with a naval bicorn hat on his bald head, indifferent to the wind, rain or heat. He arrived to offer his services for odd jobs in Ganthier and Croix-des-Bouquets, since his sheep provided only a paltry income, given that they took their time to be born, grow, give milk and die—preferably at the abattoir. Aïda took the notes and placed them into a satchel, convinced that this was all she needed to do before she quit visiting strangers' homes. She left the mysterious papers inside her bag for days, without quite forgetting them, until Timoléon came less than a week later to claim what he was owed.

Incapable of differentiating the two, Aïda asked him which note was for him and which one was for Lorénel.

'They are for the two of us,' Timoléon replied. 'All they needed was a discreet and innocent hand to distribute them.'

Indifferent to his riddle, Aïda presented him with one of the sealed papers.

The next day, she brought the second to its intended recipient. Inside Lorénel's home, standing behind the table and chair—which struck her as unnecessary, given how brief she expected her task to be—Aïda soon realized she was caught up in something beyond her control. Lorénel insisted on buying tobacco. Aïda was not there to make a sale. All the same, she unloaded the little that she had, handed him the note marked 'Duels', finished her goblet of drinking water, and then stood up to leave. 'Stay,' Lorénel said, 'Tell me a story, I could really use one.'

Without fully grasping what seemed to her an extreme farce, Aïda briefly mounted the interior horses of silence. Then, with nothing but sober generosity, she invented the story of King Kabou, a great tyrant in the eyes of the Eternal, who led an army of raving lunatics prepared for war. King Kabou believed he could manipulate the martial crowd to satisfy his desires, indulging their whims as though serving a god by provoking battles to appease them. It took him a lifetime of leadership to realize that his soldiers and various army chiefs did not wage wars for him and his sombre desires, but out of pure love of warfare and preying on the enemy. So, the king called on all his wisemen, listened to them long and hard, and found a solution to his problem which was, strangely, to subject his troops at least once to his tyrannical will without their personal commitment. He pondered day and night, concocting all sorts of pleas, calls for suicide, infanticide and other gratuitous plots of murder without enemies. He endured the most profound solitude of kings, recognizing that there was nothing more grievous than soldiers unable to meet his demands, since their own wilful servitude entailed living under ferocious and cruel royalty. Then, he decided to change strategies and came up with the simplest of plots. King Kabou loved Malika, promised to him by the neighbouring monarch, so he induced his soldiers to fight to bring her to him, inverting their love for war into a war for love. This was how his soldiers, more amenable to honour than any other human emotion, chose not to stick to their guns. They refused to fight. King Kabou's last battle was fought without weapons, fanfare or trumpets, leading his recalcitrant officers to war with only the love for love itself.

Lorénal applauded with both hands at the end of the story, as though Aïda had just walked a tightrope between two trees.

He paid her a handsome sum, considering the modesty of his home and asked her to continue doing what she was doing. 'A great deal depends on it,' he said. All she would have to do was exchange little notes between farmers, tell them whatever she liked, sell tobacco and then leave. Speaking of which, he handed her four other pieces of yellowing paper to deliver to four other farmers and a final one to return expressly to the storyteller Dorilien.

*

For several weeks, Aïda found herself ensuring the exchange of these discreet letters, without ever thinking of opening one. She became so caught up in the game that she returned disappointed if her hosts showed no particular interest in her visit. She was expected to arrive, sit down, drink some water or coffee, tell whatever story she liked, present her merchandise, deliver the message and, finally, pocket her benefactor's sum, which seemed far too generous and had nothing to do with the price of tobacco.

Look at the young girl, sitting calmly on her hosts' verandah or in their yard, waiting for someone to ask, 'Oh Aïda, what will you be telling us today?,' waiting to recite the story of the seven beauties, the seven horrors and the most wonderful marvels of the world. The children would often request her calm performance in the absence of their parents, who were busy in the fields. Sometimes, at nightfall, the adults would choose which story she should tell. There was always someone yearning for the privilege of hearing that things did not begin the way they are now, the way we see them, and to learn how one thing led to the other from the dawn of time to the present day. Satan and the three dogs waited for her outside, without leashes, trying to listen and guess which story she was telling. The days went by faster than the moments that comprised them because of a simple kind of happiness that anchored itself to this period of joyous emulation. Storytelling.

Aïda, the one for whom telling stories, having been heard, had always been a precious commodity, the one who had seen her days pass by behind the gates of silence, effaced by the reality of things standing before her, without becoming more talkative in the course of her quotidian existence, now claimed this moment of sale to explore and bring to blossom everything that had been planted inside her since the beginning: by her mother, her mother's mother, her ancestors from sable Africa, from the America of the freebooters and buccaneers, from the Atlantic Ocean, the Caribbean basin, the Antillean archipelago, from rustic Europe and the mythical Indies, through long sleepless nights where she combined the beginning of one story with the middle of another, and the end of one with the beginning of a third. And so, the story of Ti Jean, who discovered the underground spring to the delight of his village, also became the tale of Ti Jean who saved the sorceress from her evil ways, and, by doing so, returned her to the peaceful and sometimes charitable life of men. Likewise, the story of Tezen, the fish who loved the farmer's daughter by the lake, was also the terrible tale of the fish that devoured men, abducted young girls and buried them alive.

The exchange of notes and stories occupied a large part of Aïda's afternoons, drawing her away from the care that she had recently been giving Ludovic Possible. Every third evening, she paid Dorilien a visit to receive new instructions, learn about new farmers to visit and run a few errands. They spoke almost as equals. Arriving at his house, Aïda left any timidity she had at the door, and they greeted each other as though she had lived there all along. Altagrâce, Dorilien's wife, waited and hoped to see Aïda every afternoon, even when her visit was unannounced. If one day Aïda arrived without notice, in her heart of hearts, Tagrâce, like a child, was convinced that her anticipation alone had brought about this fortunate occurrence. This gave her even more reason to wait eagerly for Aïda's next visit. They did little together beyond greeting and watching each other, smiling for no apparent reason behind Dorilien's back, as if at his expense. This essential yet circumspect bond opened to Aïda the cautious and subversive circle of women in the plain as she rushed into her own reputation as a predestined renn chantrèl.

It was at this very moment that Ludovic Possible felt his new daughter, along with the rest of the world, slipping from his grasp, and quietly set in motion his plans to die.

15

Monday morning. As he dipped his bread into his coffee to spare himself the effort of chewing, Ludovic Possible acknowledged his weariness with living. Before finishing the second cup of his beloved beverage, he outlined, point by point, the terms of his will.

That Thursday evening, after a round of dominoes and abandoning the other players on the verandah, Ludovic asked Aïda to accompany him inside. He inched along with his walking stick and entered the house, where Paloma Placide sat at the table in the middle of the room. In the presence of Pépé the Tempest, Ludovic announced that Aïda was, henceforth, the proprietor of three hundred and sixty plots of adjacent farmland, dozens upon dozens of livestock, and of several rental contracts at Tapage Market. More still, as for his supplementary possessions, Aïda would oversee their distribution among the other children and grandchildren, but only in the event of an inheritance claim upon his death, and in accordance with an allocation decided by her, the sole arbiter. There was only one catch: if the death of the testator occurs, as intended, prior to the twenty-first birthday of the beneficiary, Aunt Placide will hold the property rights in her capacity as guardian and executor of the will until Aïda reaches legal maturity, and to whom it may concern. With the will as a fait accompli, Ludovic embarked on his first attempt to die.

'I shall die next Saturday,' he declared to Aïda, who did not reply.

However, during her round the next day, Aïda told Désirée about it, who told Gibril Cador, who informed Bérénice, Timoléon, Brother Lélé and Mama Résia, who, in turn, informed every passer-by everywhere, in every nook and cranny of the Cul-de-Sac plain. On the Saturday in question, they were all prepared, including Frankel Bontemps, the elderly undertaker, and Sèvila Maîtresse-Caye, mother to some of the undertaker's children, but also someone who is particularly weepy, known far and wide for the power of her voice and the empathy of her wailing. Only Ludovic was unaware that the word of his foretold death had already made the rounds in Croix-des-Bouquets.

At the beginning of Saturday afternoon, he lay in bed as though for a nap, waiting for the self-fulfilling prophecy. He sank into a deep sleep and began to tread the calm, woeful path towards death. He could already make out a few of his friends and acquaintances from times long past. He saw the old Luc Montagnier, from when he had lived on Rue Sainte-Honoré in Paris, a member of the Society of the Friends of Black People and Abbé Grégoire's close friend. Luc constantly told him, 'My friend, the only little thing that those of your race lack is having been born with the light hair of the Holy Spirit. Besides, as men, I daresay you are just as intelligent, my dear boy, just as intelligent as any white man.' Ludovic saw the rails of the ship that brought him back to Port-au-Prince, and the old one-armed admiral who claimed to have four children by four different negro women. Little sang-mêlés, those mixed-bloods, the admiral delighted, but they were not bastards, they all bear my name, and, as sons of a white man and free Black women, this land of Saint Domingue belongs to them. Ludovic Possible was on the verge of seeing the priest from his first communion at the Parish Church of Cap Haïtien, already distinguishing his heavy cassock, when Sèvila's first wail cut his interior voyage short.

Ludovic woke up furious. What on earth is wrong with this country where, after nearly eighty years of relentless giving, one cannot even die in peace? What is this land where ill-intentioned peasant women show no respect at all for eternal rest? Ludovic saw his plans thwarted, postponed until more favourable circumstances arose.

'Get out of my sight,' he scoffed at the crowd, 'troublemakers, killjoys! The people around here will smother you to death with attention!'

Some said that Ludovic was now like a wise tree that had lost its leaves; others claimed that he must have made a pact with the devil. Everyone agreed to grant him peace and to leave him alone with his fatherless daughter, in their absurd, lonely, misplaced filiation. They also say that Papa Possible left behind in the great beyond the part of the soul that contained his personality—his *bon zanj*. Since that evening, he had spoken mostly about people that only he could visualize, constantly invoking the time before his thirties—a time when a person's world was predetermined by the colour of their skin and their age, and when survival was proportional to one's capacity to inflict death. In short, this renaissance of the good old days in Papa Possible's mind did not prevent him from retaining a certain degree of lucidity—foggy, yes, but still functional.

*

A week later, Aïda still hadn't fully understood what had just happened to her. The drivelling of adults, she must have thought, had no artistic quality whatsoever. Better to pursue the agreeable quotidian of a fool for hire. However, the change in her host's tenor made her envision a journey with no return, as if, unbeknownst to her, by continuing to walk with her eyes fixed on the horizon, she would be thrust onto a new path. She made her way to the home of Émilia and Maléa, two ageless women of O'Gorman who lived together, did everything together, and would perhaps even die together. The pair was always seen at Tapage Market, selling their wares according to the day or the season—one completing the other's sentence or responding in the other's place, as though they shared a single thought between two mouths. Many contradictory truths swirled around the two women, who neither confirmed nor ever denied them. They say that one is a widow, that the other wed a man whom she never saw after their wedding night—he disappeared between the sheets early the next morning. They say that the women are companions, femmes-compères, that one a man and the other his dearly beloved, with no one knowing where they have come from or where they are going. After their conversation with Aïda in their yard, just as they were paying for the tobacco, there was a moment of hesitation. Émilia's reluctance was palpable, her brows raised, and out of respect, she could not bring herself to extend her hand to pay someone wealthier than herself.

It just so happened that the land where the commères' household stood—where they toiled with the seasons and braved their own distress—despite its distance from Boën, now belonged to Aïda. Since words have no bodies by which to travel, only speed, in less than a week, Aïda, without realizing it herself, was no longer the same person. Those who knew the secret of her lineage—that is, nearly everyone—had already conjured the image of another, even more powerful and intimidating Aïda, projected onto the flesh of the young tobacco seller. This new reality complicated the plans of Big-Bellied Dorilien and Timoléon Jean-Baptiste, who had, no doubt, made Aïda a key accomplice in their rebellious plot. Aïda sensed what might be coming for her. Aïda was sad. Aïda was alone.

*

At this portentous moment, a young and newly appointed emissary arrived in the parish of Croix-des-Bouquets—a sworn official and ordained priest by the name of Nestor Poil. The old parish of Croix-des-Bouquets, established nearly a century ago in 1750, had, every three years, always welcomed a young itinerant priest, aware of his evangelical civilizing mission and eager to extend a hand to savages in the hopes of leading them, if possible, to the light and fullness of divine communion. Like many emissaries of God before him, Nestor Poil had heard that the vast plain of Cul-de-Sac, in the west of the young Haitian nation, concealed mysterious places where supernatural roosters grew to the size of a human at night, when no one was looking. Places where time-honoured veterans of the war for national independence lived to the age of three hundred, so that, from one generation to the next, they could witness their children and grandchildren wither under the eternal curse of their victory and the freedom won from the former pro-slavery metropoles.

Among all the superstitions that the priests brought with them, Nestor Poil was particularly struck by the accounts that an arcane tribe of sorcerers abounded in those parts. Beings that existed somewhere between the sorceress and the nightingale, between Pico della Mirandola, knower all things, and the Pied Piper of Hamelin from thirteenth-century Germany—enchanters like those who, during the Holy Roman Empire until the end of Charles IV's reign, charmed the young masses with their music, only to lead them from their homesteads down the road of damnation. This band of sorcerers told simple tales whose powers compelled people to rebel against the natural order of things: the Church, the Family and the State.

Nestor Poil was a savant of his time. He was convinced that the island of Haiti was home to tribes whose customs were more or less savage, more or less African, depending on whether European Christianity or Franco-Spanish colonization had succeeded, or failed, in guiding them down the right path. Still, he was certain of one thing: the true, hidden face of these peasants did not lie in the three cults discussed by other scholars: the Moundélé, the rite of work; the Bafioté, the rite of hospitality; and the Doquila, the rite of bounty and charity. He knew that these rural folk were captivated by an ancient beast. Just as in the

Holy Bible, one thousand eight hundred years before them, the peasants of Ayiti Chérie, also called Ayiti Toma, were enthralled by the serpent and the snake—reptiles favoured by the Devil—and venerated, in the name of Vodou, the spirit of everything that slithered on the ground, never raising their eyes to the heavens. Arriving in Croix-des-Bouquets on a sweltering Saturday afternoon, he carried an apostolic brief appointing him to observe, aid and promote the spread of the gospel of Jesus Christ in the most remote reaches of the young and bellicose nation. Truth be told, based on this brief, he had no real understanding of the true scope of his eventual mission.

The day after his arrival, Nestor Poil was sipping his morning coffee when he was informed of a man crucial to his mission—someone with intimate knowledge of the local terrain, having served as the agent responsible for the census. This was particularly important to Nestor, as, in keeping with his civilizing mission, he had no desire to tarry about in the town centre, where the news of eternal grace was already well known. He wished to venture into the remote wilderness, far from the roads, into the demon's den, to understand those resistant to faith, help them, and guide them towards divine reason. His host readily agreed. Yes, there are people in these lands resistant to progress, the true enemies of religion and the nation. They lie and betray the people. They wilfully manipulate scarcity to better subjugate the sharecroppers. They invent imaginary figures, feed every superstition and suppress reason in favour of the adoration of fetishes. These people deserve punishment: imprisonment, seizure of their property and strict re-education of their children in good manners.

Nestor Poil was disarmed by the impertinence of his guest. The gentleman did not even wait for him to invent a meaning for his mission before enlisting him for a punitive expedition. The guest seemed to know exactly whom Nestor Poil was referring to and proceeded to enumerate everyone's capital sins. His calm demeanour contrasted sharply with his fiery words.

Nestor Poil showed him out, saying:

'I am Father Poil, Nestor Poil, and I shall take my time observing everything up close, following your valuable advice.'

'I am Balthazar Possible, your humble servant in eradicating the bad seeds.'

*

Then and there, Balthazar learnt that Ludovic had created a will and, out of complete disregard for years of his accumulated advice, Ludovic chose to leave everything that belonged to him to the girl—even though it was Balthazar alone who could truly ensure the family's wealth would continue to flourish. He knew, with painful clarity, that this had happened without so much as a ripple, without anyone even considering if Balthazar had something to say. Could he not, by law or by right, expect to leave some land to his own children and grandchildren? Not even Désirée, his own daughter, could speak up—making a mockery of the famous words of Jean-Jacques Dessalines, the founder of the Haitian nation, who had reclaimed the land for the descendants of enslaved Black people. Désirée could have at least said something along the lines of: 'My poor father, isolated in all of Croix-des-Bouquets—will he have nothing after all these wrongs you've made him endure? Will he have no say in the redistribution of assets?' But Désirée said no such thing. While no line of succession allowed Ludovic to claim what Balthazar had toiled away at for years, according to paragraph one, nothing in the will gave Balthazar enough grounds to contest Ludovic's declaration. So, it is true, all the land left behind will belong to Aïda—now also a Possible—and to her alone. Especially if, as stated in the second and final paragraph Ludovic, in his role as notary, had the final say on what belonged to whom and under what terms.

Finally, for the record, it should be noted that Balthazar held a few modest land titles in the neighbouring countryside, over which he retained final authority. But even so, this nameless vexation only added to the already long list of public affronts that he had to swallow. Waiting for a clearer plan, his vague idea was to invalidate Ludovic Possible's property titles, undoing Aïda's inheritance, thereby, making himself the owner of all of the assets. Then, if he had to, he would draw up his own testament in favour of Aïda without the slightest change in disposition or proportion.

After the meeting with Father Poil, Balthazar sent his friend Luiz Hernando Santana to roam Boën.

'Go back home to the east, my dear friend,' he said. 'Things are going to get unpleasant on this side of the island.'

16

Since the tragic beheading of the Vile Beast, Luiz Hernando no longer left Balthazar alone to himself. Having rejoined him later that evening, they ground their teeth for two days, then left together for Croix-des-Bouquets, abandoning Boën to the poor weather ahead. They undoubtedly wanted to wait it out in silence, pondering the best way to avenge their rooster and to restore Balthazar's honour. Perhaps they secretly hoped, especially Luiz Hernando, that someone would come to speak with them, that another would flatly apologize and a third would bring them all that they were owed from the bets. But no one ever came. The residents of Boën continued living their lives without them. In Croix-des-Bouquets, they stayed at a seasonal residence for travelling merchants, which, from Balthazar's perspective, was like suffering martyrdom all the while wallowing in shame. Every night, as proof of his frigid rage, Balthazar reported all of the happenings in the plain to Luiz Hernando. Given the rarity of his outings, that information was gathered from within the confinements of his lively bedroom walls. While urging Luiz Hernando to return home, Balthazar asked him to make a stop in Boën to collect, on his behalf, the earnings from the bets, including profits and subsidiary fees. Together they drew up a list of the farmers and their obligations, the terms and total sum of each debt. To ensure that Luiz Hernando had some skin in the game, Balthazar added:

'Of course, my friend, you shall guard the purse. You will send it back to me, if necessary, when your brothers stop wanting to tear our island in two.'

No sooner said than done, Luiz Hernando set his sights for Boën. A man with a taste for money, he did not linger for a single moment to reflect. He had no doubt that his friend Possible would reveal to him, a Spanish-speaker of the house, Santana, a revolutionary name throughout the east, to be in business with the residents of the countryside. Once he was settled in Balthazar's home, he began making his rounds among various debtors. Some received him with hostility, others with indulgence, but nobody would give him a penny. At last he reached the home of Timoléon Jean-Baptiste, who happened to be out. He came upon Commère Bérénice, who told him, without raising her voice:

'Of course, Luiz, if you were not as idiotic as the gourde you so adore, you would have realized that at this very moment you are being pursued by every soldier in the area. So you wish to ally us with the east of the island, and you are gathering funds to support a secession . . . '

It was true that, since the beginning of the year 1842, the militant separatists in Santo Domingo were becoming increasingly radicalized against Port-au-Prince. They complained that, in order to pay the independence debt, the government had been tightening the screws of injustice against the east more than anywhere else in the country. They were being unceremoniously bled dry. They only had two deputies, despite the vast territory they represented, in a Parliament that only spoke to them in French, never in their beautiful Spanish tongue. They claimed they were forced to close schools and universities. They endured such austerity that they could no longer pay the local functionaries and soldiers sent by Port-au-Prince since the unification of the island in 1822. They had impoverished themselves to such an extent that they believed they could do better on their own, without the assistance of the western side of the island, which was supposed to protect them from British, Spanish and North American imperialism. Nevertheless, they sought allies throughout the countryside, and every form of support was welcomed in the name of emancipation. It was not uncommon to witness people here and there inciting a widespread peasant uprising while gathering resources to finance their own movement.

Luiz Hernando, who had not seen things in this regard, tiptoed out of Bérénice Jean-Baptiste's home, without a word of thanks and without closing the small wood gate behind him as he exited her yard. He set his course for his own country, feeling suddenly less concerned about the fate of the west and its inhabitants. He kept moving forward, without looking back, without any regret or bitterness, until he arrived at the far reaches of the Ozama, on the southeastern end of the island, in Santo Domingo, where he landed at the treasury and the tax collector's office, in keeping with his family destiny and its inalienable ties to money.

*

Balthazar learnt of Luiz Hernando's flight with a certain sense of relief. Though he had singled Luiz Hernando out and alerted the troops to his presence in Boën, he did not wish for his only friend to be captured by Haitian soldiers hunting separatists. Instead, he wanted to point the finger at Boën as a suspicious place, the proving ground for unrest. He liked poor old Santana, his gambling disciple. Moreover, since Luiz Hernando had not been captured, there would be no other version of the events—Balthazar Possible was the only one who could explain to the political authorities the dispute between the peasants and the strange Dominican. He could divulge, hand on his heart, which peasants supported the separatist rebellion and which did not.

*

These recent events passed faster than the season that carried them. The late summer, an interminable September, dragged on, reinventing itself without a single drop of rain glistening in the sky for some time. Although not long ago, the last flood loosened its grip in people's memories. It had become ancient history, a time when the gods had a peculiar way of expressing their disdain towards the earthworms. Nowadays, everything was grey under the reign of His Majesty, the dust. The younger generation had learnt why the water passing through Boën was called the White River: it was little more than a wide path of white gravel, over which meandered a rivulet of tired water. The peasants would come and draw water for their survival, but the possibility of damming it caused such conflict that no one dared to say: 'Let us dig here and dam the water there, or irrigate this way so that certain plants remain protected despite the drought.'

It was so hot that the ground appeared to recoil. The soil cracked, sending bits of sand flying without any wind noticeable to humankind. It was a dry, continental heat, so intense that the women and men of Boën, accustomed to the usual thick island heat, found themselves gobsmacked, as if caught in an evil spell. Far from the habitual torpor of this time of the year, this particular heat brought an oppressive energy: everyone moved and tired just as quickly, as though forced to live in a prolonged, stubborn sense of urgency.

Following Balthazar's encounter with Nestor Poil, Luiz Hernando's jaunt in the countryside, and his alerting of the soldiers stationed in Croix-des-Bouquets that disturbing elements were afoot in Boën, he resumed the census of the peasantry, which had previously been hindered by none other than Balthazar himself.

During the last census attempt, carried out under the fiery authority of the young rural commandant Pierre Saurel, the few peasants who participated invented lines of filiation: claiming that they had no children despite having as many as seventeen, swearing that they had no brothers or sisters, or even that they did not know their own mother's name. They were not allowed to recount their dreams to the census agent, as they had with Ludovic Possible. In the beginning, they resisted almost out of indignation, not understanding why a complete stranger had arrived with his notebook, intent solely on recording their names. They imagined all sorts of things. Perhaps, they thought, if the French were to re-establish slavery, they would begin by counting the labour force. Or maybe the census aimed to expand another type of forced labour, the corvée, which was not the same as slavery: since those subjected to it worked, were mistreated and unpaid, yet still remained free. Then, another rumour started circulating, that the count was for capitation, an old form of per-person taxation, *one tariff per individual,* lost in the meanderings of European History, yet still practised by the neighbouring United States. Capitation meant everyone had to pay a fixed amount for simply existing, regardless of wealth or poverty. Naturally, that was why everyone needed to be accounted for.

To keep any of those possibilities from happening, the locals deployed their entire bag of tricks. Some pretended they were drunk morning to night. Others acted like they were deaf and mute. Everyone was in complete solidarity, and after all this, the census agents themselves, the rural commandant and his two aides-de-camp, forgot why they had been there and how to account for their work. For better or worse, they remained ensconced in the area until Pierre Saurel, esteemed nephew of District Commandant Éric Saurel, decided to eat a coconut and fell from the top of one of the two coconut trees designated for public use.

*

The truth is that the soldiers could very easily have extracted the names of every local—including first names, marital status, number of children and even meals they eat in a year—with a few blows of their batons to the kidneys. That is, if Balthazar had not been the protector of the countryside at the time. One can imagine Commandant Saurel's surprise when Balthazar Possible burst into his office and declared:

'I will officially assume the title of rural officer and section chief.'

According to Article 120 in the rural code, the officer of the rural police is a deputy and guarantor of the country's national order. He reports to the District Commandant, who reports to the President of the Republic. He carries out his duties in harmony with the Council of Notables and follows the recommendations of the Justices of the Peace. If the Section Chief is also a Justice of the Peace, the combination grants him absolute authority, since he both asserts and secures his own power.

'Boën will become a proper military town,' Balthazar added, 'and, Lord willing, it will be made a parish.'

'So be it,' Éric Saurel replied, taking the time to gather himself. 'So be it.'

'I will show them, those ill-mannered negroes, and they will learn some respect.'

Éric Saurel received Balthazar's volte-face with a certain degree of relief. He could have anticipated much worse, and since his nephew's death, he had not completely given up on attempting a new census. He was prepared to name, certify and do all the rest by virtue of the powers vested in him—when Balthazar added, unexpectedly:

'I shall also be the new notary. There are many matters that need to be reviewed and verified over there.'

Éric Saurel, woe was he, did not have the courage to protest—two notaries were one too many. He could also not bring himself to articulate that three ranks in one—rural officer, justice of the peace and notary—contradicted not only every legal precedent but also the freedom they normally ensured. Too tired to fuss over procedure, Commandant Saurel mumbled to himself: 'Better two notaries than none at all, I suppose.' Knowing nothing about the Possibles, he took out his inkwell and quill. 'Here stands Balthazar, registered notary in charge of the census, authorized to lead personnel and to bring a vicar with him, as necessary, to establish a parish.

'There is one more thing,' Balthazar announced.

At this point, the old commandant felt his stomach drop to his knees, as if two invisible hands were clutching his shoulders. Panic seized him.

'There is one more thing—you are coming with us, and you will bring your beasts along, too.'

*

A veteran of the War for Independence, Éric Saurel heroically fought at Vertières, the November 1803 battle that witnessed the debacle of the Napoleonic Army against the Indigenous Army of Haiti. Among the most valorous soldiers in his garrison were a few hounds that he had raised and trained himself, following a plurisecular colonial technique for taming canines. His beasts must have devoured so many French asses that he could no longer feed them anything but fresh, bloody meat. He maintained this old custom, feeding successive generations of dogs with raw meat, preparing them to defend the motherland against the next white incursion. Thirty-nine years later, he was the owner and trainer of two brown hounds who watched over his later years. The pending payment of the independence debt did not discourage him because, as he often said, our fathers the whites are a hundred times more cunning than the rest of us bourgeois mulattoes. If they think they can play a bait-and-switch on us and retake this country won at such a cost of blood, there will be a bayonet at their throats. That is how we shall treat them.

In truth, Éric Saurel was nothing more than an old man, tired and exhausted, living off a military pension that he handsomely padded with the soldiers' share of tax revenue, which he exchanged for canteens of alcohol, burning his throat from morning to night. Of course, he had the two dogs in his yard, fed them the same diet of fresh meat, and made sure they were well trained and exercised regularly. Yet the commandant's lassitude influenced everything around him, including his hounds, still very young in dog years, which had adapted to the beat of their master's drum to the point of indulging in their own alcoholic indiscretions. Sometimes, Éric Saurel was so inebriated that he confused waking life with somnolence, finding himself in a fantastical dream of a revolutionary battle. He could be heard shouting nightly: 'Long live Capoix-La-Mort! Long live Jean-Jacques Dessalines! Attack!' As though he were reliving Vertières *ad vitam aeternam*, over and over and over. At seventy-five well-counted years, he appeared older than he was—a sorry sight, perhaps, if he were not still at the helm, which meant that almost no one dared to look.

*

Balthazar Possible brought along great men of calibre to reconquer Boën. The entourage was so imposing that Nestor Poil, plagued by doubts, asked for them to clarify the role that God would play in the coming expedition. Father Poil wished to serve a cause. He wanted to guide his companions on a mission of spiritual discovery, the civilizing aims of which extended beyond merely erecting a presbytery chapel and perhaps one day—why not—with the assistance of God the Holy Father, and even the occurrence of an act of canonization, the construction of a church. But he, Father Poil, knew just how long and complex the process would be. Motivated by these personal goals, he harboured no illusions about first contact, hoping instead to be surprised and, at the same time, to anticipate what would come next.

'It is up to the Lord to guide our steps,' Nestor Poil told Balthazar, who hardly asked for more.

Having never been Christian a day in his life, Balthazar knew that biblical precepts and the inhabitants of the plain were two separate elements, and that all that was necessary was to expose one to the other, thereby sowing the beauteous disorder of reconquest summoned by his woeful designs.

17

Less than a week later, Balthazar returned with a horde of sixty-odd people, including twenty-five soldiers and one priest. After five days, his henchmen seized Aïda when she was on her merchant round. Soon, they would come for Ludovic Possible himself, no longer master of his own land.

At the critical stage of the expedition, Balthazar had hoped to find his house in supreme dignity. He had loaded a cart drawn by four cattle, saddled six horses and four mules, not to mention the donkeys each person on foot had also laden. He largely helped himself to the stores of foodstuffs that were regularly replenished by the farmers who had long been promised participation in the Exposition universelle. They had been told to submit a sample of produce for a non-existent jury of hand-picked nobles. Balthazar stockpiled dried fruits, tubers and green vegetables; he loaded up salted pork, goat and dried beef, sheep and poultry, then set out with a company composed of soldiers under the orders of the acting captain, Commandant Éric Saurel. The distance from Croix-des-Bouquets to Boën varies, depending on whether one cuts diagonally across the fields or ventures from one plantation to the next. He made his rounds to the landowners' residences as often as possible, thereby conforming to the missionary allure of his improbable trek. Having left with only the soldiers and the priest, he recruited peasants at every stage, giving the journey a new purpose and an entirely different scope.

There were about thirty voluntary recruits, among them enemies of Ludovic Possible. Some had nothing else to do, and others, intrigued by the prospect of receiving food every day in exchange for their participation, thought that joining the incursion was not at all an unappealing idea. There was also an entire family—wife, husband and children—so far in debt, who sincerely believed their bodies and souls belonged to the Possibles, that they had no qualms about following one Possible in preparation for attacking the other. As for the priest, the commandant and the twenty-five soldiers, they formed an inquisition that fabricated a cause within a few days by the mere fact of its assembly. The inquisition would choose targets indiscriminately, hoping to suppress nocturnal gatherings, nuisances to the public order, plots against the safety of the State, and known bands of wrongdoers—everything personified by Ludovic Possible and Timoléon Jean-Baptiste. Not to mention the young girl and illegitimate heir, Aïda, and the storyteller and lodyanseur Big-Bellied Dorilien, both guilty of animist accounts and of severe idleness against the good Christian faith and the explicit obligation to till the soil.

*

Aïda deviated her gaze from the path ahead. She noticed six men in uniform ordering her—shouting—to control her dogs. Sniffing the soldiers and sensing their intentions, Ti Beau, Le

Maître and Le Grand started to growl and readied themselves for battle. Never before had any unusual scent ever posed a threat as Aïda went about selling tobacco and telling her stories. Except for that late afternoon: the dogs snuffled instead of listening to Aïda tell tales. It was their cold muzzles that would lead them down an unexpected path. The soldiers were right in front of the dogs, face to face, asking Aïda and her companions to follow them without causing any trouble. Ti Beau was still grumbling, but Aïda managed to calm him down with, 'That's all right, my sweet doggie,' and then asked the soldiers to release Satan the donkey laden with her stock, because it had nothing to do with this. Aïda moved closer to her destiny, following the orders of her captors, very curious to see what would happen next.

They did not take Aïda to the military post that Balthazar's residence had become, but to the small house where she had lived with her poor mother, Gracilia France Placide. Once there, Aïda was asked to leave all her belongings outside. They confiscated her satchel containing snuff, two or three of Dorilien's sealed notes, the plan for the week and a few other objects—probably a couple of tiny figurines so long forgotten that she could barely identify them. Before entering the verandah, a fat-nosed soldier handed Aïda a leash with three woven ends. Aïda's heart leapt as she considered the indignity of not only finding herself a prisoner but also tied up in her childhood home. More than indignation, it recalled a particular nightmare—after her mother's death, when the walls had closed in on her like a casket and she had to resist with all her strength not to be shut away. However, this nightmare, at least, was completely different, because the soldier told her:

'You cannot expect us to tie up your filthy mongrels!'

Reluctantly, under duress, Aïda made a knot around Le Grand's neck and another around Ti Beau's. Meanwhile, Le Maître, aware of his fate and unaccustomed to the yoke, instinctively bolted in the direction of freedom—the highway. The two other dogs were tied to a lemon tree in the back of the yard. Aïda entered the prison that was once her house, which she found almost empty: a mat waiting for her in one corner, and in the other, a second mat supporting the sprawling paunch of a resting man. Aïda had stumbled upon Big-Bellied Dorilien, her cellmate.

Dorilien woke up to explain his own journey.

A few hours earlier, he had been peacefully devoting himself to his afternoon activities—tending to his roosters, preparing for a siesta—when three men showed up in his yard. They threatened him with a bayonet and forced him to follow them outside. Altagrâce, upon seeing her husband being escorted away by these scarcely affable individuals (and that is the least we might say), leapt into the yard with her bare hands ready to kill or be killed. Once she stood before the men, she had no chance to launch into fisticuffs, halted instead by the calm, almost smiling visage of her orator-husband. 'Tagrâce, these men are old friends. When the time comes for you to go looking for us, you will find us at Balthazar's house.' That is how, by mistaking the destination, Dorilien found himself in Aïda's old home, where he honoured the hour of the siesta with the greatest of ease until she arrived. This is also why Tagrâce was not there, ready to defy the entire country so that her man would not have to go to bed elsewhere without a story to tell, and so that his newfound friend Aïda might not bear such a sombre past into her young adulthood.

*

Because they were entitled to no respite, Aïda and Dorilien saw Balthazar Possible appear in the flesh in what was now their prison. He emerged suddenly, like an apparition, accompanied by four soldiers armed with batons. The military greys and epaulettes suited Balthazar well, like the most sophisticated fashion. He stood firm, his rifle draped across his back with a bandolier, and stated Article 180 of the rural code, which stipulated that every inhabitant of the countryside must have an occupation relating to the soil and that, of course, there was no place for idleness in any form whatsoever, including under the auspices of blathering or prattling off those godforsaken stories all the blessed day or in the clearest of nights. Balthazar glared at Dorilien. A moment passed. 'Your filthy stories are tormenting our souls,' he added. 'And now, giant roosters pop out of your magician's hat and strut about in the streets. This is neither Christian nor legal.' While speaking, Balthazar tried with all his strength not to look towards Aïda. He did not utter a word against her because, besides the pain of having to detain her, something clasped at his throat simply at the sight of this child who had once been almost like one of his own. This 'something' might have been shame.

Dorilien remained seated on his mat for Balthazar's entire speech, during which he revealed he knew every line of Dorilien's notes by heart. Balthazar interpreted his strange correspondence as a call for insurrection, an explicit incitement of civil war. Not least because of the inscription *Duels* on the cover of the folds, which, even without an exclamation mark, seemed to invoke that injunction [a verb] belonging to what we call the third person singular. The word 'Duels', so crisp and powerful, capable of evoking a poetry so simple yet militant, acted as the pièce de resistance of a scarcely veiled political plot.

To catch his breath, Balthazar led the officers towards the exit and they followed him out as though they were his trailing odour. He attempted, once again, not to turn towards Aïda, a useless precaution since, from the moment he had entered the house, Aïda had turned on her side, staring at the wall to avoid the gaze of Balthazar, whom she pitied.

In terms of their content, the notes Aïda distributed on Big-Bellied Dorilien's behalf were composed of newspaper clippings, a few excerpts of legal documents, reproductions and brief exegeses of certain laws of the land: the rural code, every constitution since 1801, a few improbable decrees. There was also fragmentary correspondence between Port-au-Prince and Paris concerning the independence debt—records of payments made to France, records of the immediate, quantified deficit and their implications for the national budget. Occasionally, a few excerpts of speeches made before the Haitian Parliament slid their way into 'Duels'. Other times, there were pro-independence pamphlets coming from the eastern part of the country—Cibao and Ozama, in Dominican lands. Recently, one could also read Praslin's *Manifesto*, published in the southern end of the country on the first of last September, which called for a full-scale revolt, an armed overthrow of the powers that be.

Information and knowledge were the weapons that Big-Bellied Dorilien and Timoléon Jean-Baptiste placed in the hands of a few farmers in the Cul-de-Sac plain who could read and write, with the notable exception of Ludovic Possible. Not because they mistrusted him, or because, since he was a mulatto and a proprietor, they were attempting to keep him out of their business. For as long as he had lived in Boën, the villagers had learnt to forget Ludovic's status and accepted him as one of their own. Instead, since their pamphleteering was bound to erupt, they had hoped to protect their old friend from any violence he might be subjected to as a renegade, defector and traitor to the dominant race who not only wanted to educate the children of Black peasants but also let their slavish parents fiddle around with the dangerous tools of enlightenment.

In this world without even a newspaper available to the vast majority, the comparative study of the country's principal laws and statutes, taking the form of a long dialogue whispered in the woods, demonstrated to everyone the tightening belt of the coded speech that confined them to a peasant life with no future. These very words, like a rumour, wandered into their minds, making them dream that if one day they could leave, it would be to return to the very place they had left, like ants marching in a circle. For those capable of seeing through the murky waters of these unjust regulations, it was clearly stipulated that each and every farmer was forever destined to be born and die poor, deprived of dreams and a history, forbidden to leave their huts and breadbaskets for the world of cities.

*

Balthazar left the room.

He was the only one among the living who knew how much Aïda loved ripe plantains drenched in sauce, topped with kippers and ripe avocado. The avocado season had ended and, in any case, the plain produced very little. Yet, a woman arrived with a bounty of kindness, grace and Aïda's favourite food. She asked Dorilien if he had any preference for tomorrow's meal, and suggested to Aïda that, if ever, as a young girl, she longed for the company of people her own age, she could bring her daughter with her. The woman also said that the Aïda could join them outside, under the mess tent, if that would please her.

Aïda and Dorilien did not so much as bat an eye at the generous spread in the corner until, as night fell, hunger came to settle the score, looking to knock them down, even though they were already lying on their beds of straw.

The woman came once again, carrying a wick to burn. She spoke to them with such commiseration that Dorilien thought to do her a favour by finally touching the plate of food. As he began to eat, Aïda followed, and the two ate under the tender vigilance of a burning wick.

This new step towards complicity took hold late in the evening, for after they finished eating, aware of the way time would stretch its arms into the next morning, Dorilien looked at Aïda with an unbothered smile, anticipating what would come next. Aïda looked at Dorilien—dubious, hesitant, incapable of believing what he was thinking. She was timid. She lowered her head, then raised it, assuming big old Dorilien's combative attitude. Dorilien rose, pushed his straw mattress against the wall, perpendicular to Aïda's, and sat back down in complete comfort, facing the front door with his back to the wall. Aïda poured herself some water. She would have preferred a dose of tobacco since the night would be long. Thus was announced, in that bedroom slowly undulating beneath a feeble, shimmering flame, the most impressive duel to unfold in the Cul-de-Sac plain, in the entire country, perhaps even the whole world. Far more impressive than Biss the Undefeated versus the Vile Beast, and even more than the adventurous tales of the greatest knights—for ultimately this was less of a duel than a subtle joust without an audience, between friends, lost in the sombre folds of whispers: Dorilien and Aïda were going to tell each other stories.

*

Aïda had an advantage to start, for her stories never had anything to do with the audience. If she had been called to spin a tale with a loud and intelligible voice, it was as a creature of Dorilien's own making, ever since her mother's wake. So much so that, following a narrative arc as old as the world itself, a creation was to surpass its own creator. One must also not forget that Aïda was on familiar ground, within the walls of her childhood home, right where her mother introduced her to the eternal and solitary art of making imaginary beings follow the path of their destiny. The room was no longer the same, now empty and miserable: two straw mattresses and a chamber pot where she had to relieve herself twice in the presence of an adult man. Outside, the guards were not too far away, drinking and hanging about. Aïda was confident that her keepers would allow nothing in terms of her release. In these parts, everyone's notion of the world boiled down to the Cul-de-Sac plain. Yet all this—the mere presence of those walls, the shame Aïda swallowed in place of the adults, the stories she carried within her even before her birth placed her in the natural position to astound her adversary, so to speak, and to teach him that, in narration, the place from which one tells a tale is often worth more than seven hundred and seventy-seven sacks of stories.

That was also Dorilien's strength, he was happy to watch her perform, to contemplate her art, and to learn how one goes from a timid silence to crafting the most beautiful possibilities through narration. Dorilien held on to one advantage—neither his age nor his virtuosity, but his curiosity. He wanted to listen; he wanted to believe. He hoped that, when it came to stories, those told by Aïda from the Cul-de-Sac plain—one who could weave stories and conjure all sorts of things—would be the truest of them all. When it was all said and done, Dorilien hadn't been born during the last time it rained. He had also endured his own share of humiliation and misery, tenderness and abnegation. He had not always been a joyous celebrant of his own success. Searching within, he could still see the person for whom every word mattered, the one who was also made of silence and hesitation. His was the advantageous position: someone who turns a loss into a win. This was no longer a mere duel, even less a sparring match, but a silent droning of things, a blanket of words shared without warning or preamble, without a *krik!* or a *krak!*, because the *lakou* was sleeping, and this was a very good thing, since it was not a matter of stirring or entertaining the *lakou* at all.

Aïda adjusted her stance. A trace of a smile appeared on her face. The situation calmly amused her as well, then she began, in Dorilien's neck of the woods, with the well-known story of Jean the Leaf and Jean the Spirit, who lived in the countryside and, as penniless peasants, had no means nor the right to move to the city.

18

Jean the Leaf was quite content with his life as a man of the *mòn*, the hills. He asked Jean the Spirit, 'But my brother, why do you wish to go to the capital? There's nothing there for us in places like that. We don't know anyone, and nobody knows us. We're like sore thumbs, ready to get hammered at any moment, with nobody around to come to our rescue.'

Jean the Spirit did not see things that way. He said to the Leaf, 'You're as stupid as can be, can't you see how miserable our life is around here? We have no dispensary for our health, no school for our children, and we sell what we grow for such a pittance that we might as well say we give it away to the big *bachas*, the landowners who strike it rich in the cities.'

'My brother,' replied Jean the Leaf, 'I feel very comfortable living here. We have the river to bathe in and trees to nap beneath. We live close to our livestock, and all we have to do is raise a hand to pluck and gobble up a ripe mango.'

Faced with Leaf's obstinacy, Spirit no longer tried to convince him. He set out to defy his brother's objections and confront life's mysteries. After many journeys back and forth, as well as countless troubles, Jean the Spirit managed to leave for work in the cities. Once he arrived, just as brother Leaf had predicted, he was met with the gratuitous hostility of the city dwellers, daily humiliation and hardships of urban life. Hardly anyone knew him, and those who did acknowledge him did so only to mock him for his rustic manners and strange customs. He, who once had the reputation of being among the most cunning folks in the countryside, passed for one of the most idiotic in the city. His knowledge was no longer of any use to him. Everything that had been most dear to him now only retained the slightest value, and that which was most futile, things that had never mattered before, now struck him as of the highest order—so much so that he quickly became one of the city's pariahs. He ran out of money because all the savings he had set aside for his city adventures barely sufficed to feed and clothe himself for a few days. Jean the Spirit led a miserable life, but he learnt one thing: in the cities, no one is ever wrong. One must never admit defeat. One day came, the next day went. On the rare occasions when he returned to the countryside, he pretended that everything was just swell. He told everyone, especially Jean the Leaf, all the beautiful things the city had to behold. Everything he saw and everything he did became the source of his happiness. One day came, and the next day went. In time, Jean the Spirit managed to convince the entire village that the city was the finest place to live on Earth.

*

After extolling the benefits of city life, Jean the Spirit could no longer set foot in the countryside without someone coming to see him.

'Tell me, my brother,' asked one, 'what must I do to go to the city myself and make the most of all these beauteous things?'

'My brother,' quizzed another, 'my goat no longer gives me milk. If I were in the city, she would give birth every month. Since her piss isn't drinkable, you must help me get there.'

Jean the Spirit buckled beneath the weight of so many requests and entreaties. The constant pleading gave him an idea: he was going to organize a collective voyage to the city.

'Here, my brother, take this baby goat in payment for the journey.'

'Listen, my brother, I don't have any baby goats, but I have six laying hens and two Spanish roosters. I'll give them to you to pay my way to civilization.'

As the bidding on their new future in the city continued, one man offered Jean the Spirit a parcel of land, while another pledged the year's harvest. One woman offered the two cows she had inherited from her father, while another gave him her mother's old silverware. Everyone wanted to leave, and Jean the Spirit said: 'No, my dear friends, in the city, people don't pay for things in sheep and goats. I shall need piastres, gourdes, countable currency, pieces of gold or precious jewellery.'

The poor peasants stared at one another. Unaware of what they possessed or what they did not, they sold everything they had. One woman sold off her house, another gave up her wedding ring, a rare possession around those parts. The more people made the effort, the more others clung to the importance of this great journey. The pile of money had now become a sack so heavy that Jean the Spirit could not carry it alone, so he enlisted the help of his brother to transport their loot to the big city.

*

Upon arriving in the capital and seeing the slum where Jean the Spirit told him to take his sack of money, Jean the Leaf asked, 'Brother, the peasants gave up everything they had to live in a place like this?'

'No,' Jean the Spirit replied. 'Tomorrow, I'll show you where all this money will go.' And so, the next morning, Jean the Spirit purchased a great house on the main street. It had a large terrace and expensive furniture.

'Now you have a nice house,' Jean the Leaf told him, 'but it is too large for you, and it seems a little too small to receive all of the peasants.'

'Well, in fact,' replied Jean the Spirit, 'they will not be coming anyhow. When they come to visit you in prison, you will explain to them how and why people in the capital live in such large abodes on the grand avenues.'

'Why in prison?' Jean the Leaf was about to ask when the gendarmerie burst in to arrest the provincial vagabond who was troubling the worthy Jean the Spirit, a wealthy bourgeois of the big city.

The story came to a close at the moment when Jean the Leaf, the poor fellow, was carted off to prison in his village, where the country folks would learn, at their own expense, how the wealth of cities is not meant for everyone.

'In every house,' Aïda added, adopting Dorilien's style of drawing lessons from his stories, 'in every home, behind the dining room, there is a kitchen where those who are not allowed a seat at the table prepare food for everyone else.'

*

The evening followed its course and Dorilien accepted the challenge. He began his turn with an enigmatic anecdote, closer to Aïda's style. It was the age-old story of the cursed child for whom everything was see-through. He could actually see through the walls and peek into peoples' hearts. He could hear the silent pain of everything.

One day, realizing the boy's extraordinary abilities, the king bathed him in riches and placed him in a tall tower. His task was to watch the entrance to the city and describe, in the smallest detail, the intentions of those who entered. He read the hearts of strangers and described the contents of their satchels.

'This one is carrying a sharp object.'

'We shouldn't let him in,' the procurer was quick to respond.

'She has a heart full of bitterness.'

'We must question her at length.'

'This one carries profound sadness.'

'He must find consolation before returning.'

'This one is full of joy.'

'Well, he can enter.'

As time passed, the city filled with good, happy people, free of troubles.

After several years, as the regent felt old age approaching and his people could no longer perceive even a semblance of sadness, he summoned the clairvoyant, no longer a child, to ask him what he saw inside the belly of the kingdom.

The clairvoyant and the regent spoke for nights and days on end. They remade the world from head to toe and shared everything dear to their hearts. The regent spoke of his childhood, his royal adolescence and the long days of his reign. The clairvoyant spoke of his isolation, of his wealth and of the long hours spent in observation. As they spoke, they shared a feeling that neither of them, despite their power and logic, could identify. So they decided to call upon clairvoyants from other cities.

At this precise moment in the story, notice the importance of having Big-Bellied Dorilien narrate instead of Aïda Possible. He narrates in a swift, lively cadence, precise down to the millimetre, the entire parade of clairvoyants who arrive at the city: the one whose beard reached his knees and counted off his visions in song; the one who declined to explain why he was called upon and predicted every one of his patrons' behaviours so that his divinatory art was always one step ahead; the one, blind in both eyes, who could tell the exact placement of things and described them to his interlocutors without the slightest error; the one who never spoke a word without seeing it come true an instant later. As many as they were, and there were still others who came from all over, none of them was capable of telling the regent and the clairvoyant of the tower the root of the feeling that animated the two of them, the feeling they had hoped to unveil with one simple word or an explanation.

So, the regent and the clairvoyant of the tower found themselves deeply unhappy. The regent could not die in peace, and the clairvoyant could not deliver him from his torment. They dried up on the inside, with no one able to describe the feeling for them, and thus release them from their shame. For after having built a marvellous city, after having erected walls around the world's most profound beauty, after having beckoned all the happiness around while rejecting the miserable, the evil, the woeful, lame, the crooked, the harebrained, the scrawny, the portly—after having taken everything while giving nothing—victory was theirs, along with an implacable, pathetic, imperceptible, limitless and enormous shame. Even worse, the victorious keepers of the realm wallowed in the misery of having no one to whom they could confess how ashamed they were to be themselves.

The morning rose after Dorilien and Aïda had exchanged several other tales. Their trading of stories revealed the distinctiveness of their styles in a prodigious turn of events and, in the end, they experienced together, neither standing up nor lying down, a joyous whirlwind of endless, leisurely tales.

*

On the other side of Boën, the first lines of market women en route to Tapage walked with their baskets on their heads, their donkeys laden, followed by barefoot little boys, more intent on teasing the animals than helping their mothers. As they passed the bayahonda shrubs without looking in Ludovic's direction, everyone still managed a small greeting and a kind word for the old man, who had hesitantly returned to his place in the verandah. Greetings of 'Bonjour, compère' that Ludovic no longer responded except in his heart or, at times, with a slight nod. The monologue at the back of his throat had nothing to do with cordial salutations, which reveal more by its tone than dissipate the palpable tension in the air. Essentially, the inhabitants of Boën were divided into two camps: those who supported little Aïda, imprisoned at the age of thirteen, and those who had abandoned her.

Midday arrived. No longer able to tolerate the wait, feeling a mixture of curiosity and dread of his own destiny boiling in his stomach, Ludovic stood up. Feeling his way around, he grabbed his cane and envisioned the road to Balthazar's. He had barely left his yard by the time he noticed a gathering. Amid the dust, he counted six people standing and two young men seated on a large rock: Bérénice, Timoléon, Gibril, Désirée, Résia and Sèvila were standing; Jean-Zamor and Doréus were seated, deciphering the hieroglyphs traced by the wind and the dry soil next to the rock. They had been waiting since the morning for Ludovic's decision to head out. Not daring to pay him a visit, they exchanged a few brief comments, punctuated by sighs and hostile huff and puffs. 'Things cannot be this way! Everything should return to the way it was before, and any damage, if it must occur, should be quickly repaired.'

Some brought with them a few tools, pruning knives and machetes. Others brought their youth and determination. Seeing their solidarity and resolve, Ludovic Possible regained a sense of strength. He paused for an instant, looked towards them, and said:

'I'm going there alone.'

Then he started down the road. As Timoléon readied a response, the old man slowed his pace, steadied himself on his cane, raised his free hand and said:

'Especially not you, Timoléon. First, we must understand what has happened before deciding what should happen next.'

They let him to walk alone, watching him split the radiance of the sun with his pale shadow, and thought of another way to thank him.

19

At Balthazar's residence, a host of shortsighted inquisitors, soldiers and petty vigilantes buzzed about, transforming the house into what seemed to be the seat of an ancient messianic tribunal against the corrupt social order and its heretical fictions. The soldiers extended the awning over the verandah so that it covered half of the front yard where they had planted pews, like in an ecclesiastical assembly facing a raised pulpit. In front of the rows of pews, they erected a lectern made from the trunk of a palm tree, topped with a wooden board, from which Father Poil planned to deliver his Sunday sermons. Upon arriving, Ludovic could not help but think of his dilapidated schoolhouse, and the miracle that could have occurred if he, too, had a contingent of soldiers at his command. Thankfully, there were children who would soon learn about the reconstitution of what was once their school.

Ludovic made his way to Balthazar's house. Contrary to his expectations, there were neither soldiers in training, nor were there rebels running helter-skelter. There was no mob rule, nor any welcoming committee ready to nail him into the pillory. Apart from the four soldiers playing cards in the front yard who did not even throw a glance in his direction, he noticed a strange man: ageless, bent over a small notebook as though he was trying to keep his head from falling onto his legs. The man looked up at Ludovic. Ludovic looked back. Then Ludovic approached, and the man stood up. He offered Ludovic his seat while he stood, leaning against one of the verandah rails.

'I am Father Nestor Poil,' he said. Ludovic remained calm. 'Your daughter is doing quite well—I'm seeing to it personally.' Ludovic lifted his gaze towards him. 'She's not here, but in her old house.'

Silence lingered for a few moments, but it did not last. Ludovic broke it just as quickly as it had set in, asking:

'What is your business? Why are you here?'

'To understand.' said the priest. 'This is my third time coming here—to Haiti. The first time, they kept me in Port-au-Prince. There is nothing mystifying about Port-au-Prince. Some do business, others are in service, and the rest are deputies, regional representatives or some other kind of delegate. The second time, I was in the north, in Cap Haïtien. I was most intrigued by the place. It is because of Cap Haïtien that I returned, making this my third voyage in five years. I travelled to the Cap just as the horrible earthquake struck on 7 May last year. I was forced to double back. I spent a while in Port-au-Prince, then my mission became clear once more—since God was already present in Croix-des-Bouquets, I wished to go even further into the countryside. Then your brother found me, and our ideas aligned. Now, I'm here.'

'Your ideas aligned?' Ludovic repeated, his breath laboured. 'What does the alignment of your ideas have to do with this place? These are peaceful peasants—just farmers and a few of their children. You came here with your men in uniform because your ideas aligned?'

'They are not my men . . .'

Right when Father Poil was ready to declare that he, a missionary appointed by an apostolic mandate, merely cooperated with legitimate militias without ever belonging to one, Balthazar appeared in the yard, one could see him from the verandah. Ludovic and Balthazar were not surprised to see each other. Only two things betrayed their emotions: the slight sneer in the right corner of Balthazar's nose and the fain droop of his eyelids, while Ludovic bowed his head for an instant and raised it just as quickly. They met each other's gaze. As the third wheel in this conflict, Nestor Poil felt a chill run down his leg. He sensed a dampness spreading in his crotch. With a silly, indecisive smile, he watched as Balthazar, without greeting either of the men, pulled up a chair for himself.

Balthazar did not sit down. He went inside, perhaps to give a few orders, then returned, followed by the four soldiers who had been in the yard, including the one with the ample nose, his aide-de-camp. Balthazar carried a large leather-bound notebook, identical to the one Ludovic used. Balthazar opened the ledger, and there, before their eyes, stood Ludovic himself, only a little younger and darker skinned. The two brothers unwittingly reflected each other's stance, except that Balthazar, with a rifle slung across his back, was followed by four wimps in a soldier's uniform. Meanwhile, nobody had ever seen Ludovic threaten anyone with a weapon. Then, the younger brother informed the elder that he was replacing him as the notary, expressing his hope for Ludovic's full cooperation in the transfer of documents and explaining that he found it necessary to detain him long enough to discuss, in the form of a legal proceeding, the most recent turn of events.

Ludovic spent the afternoon and the night at Balthazar's as though he were an invited guest. He washed, ate supper and went to bed without any spectacle.

*

The next day, Balthazar ordered Aïda and Dorilien to be moved to his house so that they could stand trial. The four soldiers tasked with their transfer came back with a sullen-yet-calm young girl, who had not changed her clothes in three days; a resentful, stocky man, who no longer spoke much; and a streak of bad luck that might haunt them for ever. The soldier with the large nose, Francius, tormented by fear, grasped the ominous nature of the prisoner transfer. He trembled in his uniform as if the Cap Haïtien earthquake was happening right beneath his feet. Before leaving the yard, Aïda asked him, 'Allow me to set my dogs free—they have nothing to do with this,' and Francius preferred not to interfere. Aïda liberated Ti Beau and Le Grand.

Dorilien and Aïda thought that as long as they were kept inside, out of public view and unbound—albeit prevented from moving freely—their arrest might be negotiable: a scandal, an indignation that each of them hoped to resolve through the art of argumentation. Now, as some strange young men dressed in military stripes—two in front and two behind—escorted Aïda and Dorilien along the sunny path, under the haggard gaze of a few nosy Boënnais, things were taking a real, irreversible, martial turn.

The early afternoon sun pummelled the ground with a burning wind. Protected by the canopy of palms behind the lectern, Balthazar designated the four soldiers of his personal guard as the members of the military tribunal. The Altesse family, which owed a great sum of money to the Possibles, was described as the complainant and witness to the prosecution, while each of the defendants sat calmly before Balthazar, watching where he would go with this, more concerned by the suffocating heat than by the masquerade of a verdict that awaited them.

*

Ludovic Possible was accused of bootlegging, forgery, and the conspicuous appropriation of other peoples' property. Aïda and Dorilien were to answer for their animist tales, the incitement of superstitious activity, the disturbance of public order and their association with miscreants. The ground was arid, and the acrid air blew the dust into a whirlwind. Balthazar the Judge intended to open the hearing in the afternoon, based on the charges registered by Balthazar the Notary and in accordance with the arrests made—without witnesses or clemency—by Balthazar the Military Officer and Balthazar the Section Chief.

The audience took their seats. Everyone who had followed the soldiers on their expedition—the men, women and children—sat as though before a tribunal assembled for the occasion.

They were lined up on benches, one behind the other, in no particular order, while the soldiers paced aimlessly, hoping for something to happen instead of nothing at all. Against Ludovic's best advice, Timoléon and others from the small group in favour of the old man and his daughter were present to witness Balthazar's human duel.

Father Poil mingled with the crowd, speaking to everyone he could. He wanted to appear benevolent, attentive and jovial towards the unshackled, uncaged prisoners. Not so much because he accepted the legitimacy of Balthazar's arrests, nor because it served his ecclesiastical designs; he was quite simply convinced that nothing harmful could come of such a trial. Balthazar only wanted to establish his authority, he told himself, to hand out a few fines here and there—not to see anyone imprisoned or martyred. He watched Ludovic allow himself to be pushed around: sleeping in his brother's house without surveillance, eating his meals without questioning how his daughter Aïda was faring—until this morning. Nestor Poil assumed that everyone wished to relieve themselves of any responsibility for the plain, which was in complete ruin. From now on, Balthazar would have to manage everything, all the way down to the change of the seasons and the drought that had settled in.

*

Watching Aïda and Dorilien arrive, followed by four unarmed soldiers, Ludovic Possible felt dizzy more from the absurdity of the situation than from the suffocating heat. It was as though he were looking at the precipice they were all facing together, wondering precisely when they had begun their downhill slide to arrive at this point. Aïda and Dorilien, without uttering a word or turning to look in his direction, sat on the same bench where Ludovic was. The four soldiers left. Mission accomplished.

Suddenly, Ludovic stood up in protest. He had things to say. He wished to question the very legitimacy of this military tribunal. He also wanted to denounce his little brother's poor showmanship, insisting on a cock-and-bull story just to claim Aïda's future inheritance, while at the same time, boasting as the proudest man alive. Ludovic intended to pontificate on how Balthazar believed he possessed a global monopoly on humiliation, and how his little brother had staged this spectacle to dish out a hundredfold what had never happened to him. He was about to voice all of this just when his momentum was abruptly halted by a sudden uproar. Timoléon's whiny voice and Doréus's defiant screams collided with the rage of a group of peasants headed by Jean-Zamor and Gibril Cador. Everyone had come with the same goal: to bring the chaos to an end, once and for all. To end the masquerade that had been sucking the air out of Boën for three days too many, causing seeds to rot inside their fruit.

*

After the collective unrest stirred by the arrival of Dorilien and Aïda, Timoléon took it upon himself to provoke Balthazar: he stared at the empty goblet in his hands, placed it on the table, and then, without speaking directly to Bérénice, said: 'I'm headed out.'

The walkout passed quickly. Although there had not been a master plan, Timoléon Jean-Baptiste was expected to be the one to defy Balthazar. There he stood: at the same door where, at the beginning of the year, he had appeared with Biss the Undefeated under his arms, soliciting a duel by cockfight. On this day, he seemed more like an accomplice to thirty or so angry peasants. Some opposed the military regime, while others sought to settle scores with Balthazar Possible. Everyone primed like a flintlock rifle, ready for sparks to fly. Unlike last time, Timoléon no longer possessed a soldier's dignity, but his firm desire for combat did not make him any less sharp. Amid the turmoil, while defending Ludovic, a man no less mulatto than his own younger brother, Balthazar, trained his ire on the self-proclaimed justice of the plain:

'Come on out, you old mulatto jackass, and let me teach you a little something about respect!'

It was true that Balthazar planned to hold Timoléon in contempt of court, finding him guilty of every conceivable offence possible: treason, civil disobedience, a lack of respect for the law of the land, intellectual dishonesty and immorality, not to mention all the unsettled debts from the wagers placed on that memorable day when the Vile Beast devoured Biss the Undefeated.

Hearing the ruckus outside his door, Balthazar raised his head. He, too, remembered that not-so-distant day when he had set a meeting with Timoléon for a prize fight. There would be no deferral this time. Balthazar ordered his soldiers to quell the rebellion and to arrest anyone who stood between them and Timoléon Jean-Baptiste—who was guilty of assault.

20

The skirmishes at the tribunal house were turning in Timoléon's favour, as his companions were furious—and justifiably so. The soldiers appeared with little conviction, tasked with imposing an ultimatum on a group of peasants already engaged in battle. The first had barely stepped through the door when they were swarmed by the crowd. When there was no escape for the others, they realized the trouble they were in. It was already too late to attack—the jubilant peasants held them in check. None had a chance to load their gunpowder or point a bayonet. The soldiers were so outnumbered that the only injuries were on their side. Some lay motionless on the ground, bruised and battered. Others clutched their heads, the blows making them forget the futility of their presence in Boën. Still, a few did nothing at all, convinced the battle would settle itself. Of Balthazar's personal guard, two of the four had already been stabbed by Gibril Cador before they could even reach for their weapons.

Timoléon's strong, albeit improvised, brigade was almost certain of its victory when the Commandant Éric Saurel stormed in on horseback, accompanied by a battalion of twelve foot soldiers and two determined, enraged mastiffs. Commandant

Saurel's arrival had been strategically timed to allow him to launch the new census during the trial and, if necessary, he would start counting the number of peasants on the spot. Without dismounting, he plunged into the yard, followed by his perspiring company, who, alongside him, swingled truncheons at anyone within arms' reach. The presence of the horse alone, combined with the the blows, caused such chaos that most of the benches were overturned. No one could tell a soldier from a civilian. Meanwhile, instead of regrouping with their respective sides, everyone tried to strike any improvised enemy upside the head.

The disorder on display looked nothing like an organized duel. So much so that, if we take this person here, Gibril, Désirée's companion, who is beating a soldier to dissuade him from arresting him and to dodge blows himself. Or, that person over there, Timoléon, who has seized a young man to teach him good manners with a few stern slaps to the face. No, we could hardly say this is the case because what unfolds is complete panic—the kind that earns *a posteriori* the great title of a battle, but which, in the moment, is nothing more than narrative hotchpotch: inextricable nonsense in which the only ounce of reason belongs to old Ludovic who hopes to rescue his daughter, for better or worse, from the verandah of an inhospitable home. Meanwhile, the priest, Nestor Poil, overwhelmed by the pandemonium, found himself speaking in Spanish and would not stop shouting: '*Dios mio, qué pasa! Dios*—restore the calm, please, get a hold of yourselves!' However, since Éric Saurel's soldiers did not bring about the desired peace—the submission of all the peasants and the acceptance of the stalled verdict—they decided not to let matters rest.

*

The agitation that persisted resembled the grunting at the centre of a raging cockfighting ring—except this time, everyone was both a participant and a spectator, committed to the fight and responding with their own blows. Éric Saurel's soldiers were prepared to arrest Timoléon Jean-Baptiste, the disorderly rebel. Order was required in moments of disorder—a moment to be seized. Threatened by the dogs that forced some to retreat, Timoléon, surrounded deep in the yard, could no longer retaliate and prepared to surrender.

Moreover, the deafening arrival of the fair lady Paloma Placide, who burst in at Balthazar's doorstep like a clap of thunder, shook everyone. In the yard, Pépé the Tempest held two young soldiers under her arm and the collar of a third in her balled fist. All three squirmed with all their might, sweating and groaning like goats, pleading to be released at once, or they would squeal even louder, an act that would apparently carry no real consequence. Pépé freed the first two of her prey from under her arms, and they sat stiffly on an uncomfortable bench. She clung to the third like a soiled handkerchief and walked towards other young soldiers, who wisely recoiled out of her way. She roared, 'Come on, is that all you've got?', annoyed at the greenhorns who scurried away. She released her third victim, who could no longer tell if he was still on planet earth or had given up his ghost. The Tempest then turned in Balthazar's direction, shouting his name like a schoolteacher in class, 'Come here, Balthazar!' It was only at this moment, with everything unfolding so quickly, that

Balthazar realized the full extent to which Paloma Placide's pugnacious presence marked the end of the trial he had initiated according to the rules of jurisprudence and vengeance.

Paloma's accomplices too caused a stir in the court proceedings, including Désirée, whom we must not forget; along with Balthazar's own daughter, Sèvila Maîtresse-Caye; and Bérénice Jean-Baptiste, to whom Timoléon barely uttered three words this afternoon on his way out; and Altagrâce, Dorilien's wife, waiting for a unified front to free her husband from the filthy clutches of these hard times. To put mildly, an unwelcome crew trailed by a few allies, Émilia and Maléa, who were all concerned with the fate of Aïda and the others, determined to bring an end to Balthazar Possible's remonstrances. Moreover, Ti Beau, Le Maître, and Le Grand—Aïda's three pets—aided the small army Paloma had assembled.

This is the story of how the dogs joined Pépé the Tempest's horde: as soon as Aïda freed them, Le Grand and Ti Beau went in search of Le Maître to bring him back. Together, the three hounds followed the countryfolk and resolved to free their friend Aïda and her unfortunate companion, Big-Bellied Dorilien. A few moments earlier, when Paloma Placide had stormed into Boën, making her way to Bérénice's home and declaring, 'Whatever needs to happen, we have to do it now,' she could not have known that the dogs roaming there were thinking the exact same thing—of course, in canine terms. Nor had she noticed that the dogs followed the assembled group from home to home, taking up the role of rear guard—the last resort if things went awry.

*

About ten months earlier, when the humans of Boën organized the bloody battle pitting the Vile Beast against Biss the Undefeated, they brought about a duel that, by and large, went by the book—played out in the finest conditions of resentment and hostility. At the time, they could not have foreseen that the dogs would, in turn, wage war and choreograph the quickest, most unwholesome, and perhaps the most macabre episode of all.

Dogfighting is not an ordinary custom in the land of Haiti, Ayiti Toma, Quisqueya or Boyo, situated in the Antillean archipelago at eighteen degrees latitude north and sixty-two degrees longitude west, right at the mouth of the Gulf of Mexico. Instead, we have heard stories—with little proof—of how, far away, on the other side of the water, in North Carolina, some slaveholders, to amuse themselves, pitted Black people against dogs, Black people against Black people, and dogs against dogs. At another time, still without any proof beyond a few witness accounts, we learnt of two canines belonging to the Royal Company who imposed a reign of terror on a small village in the British colony of India. They decided all by themselves, without their masters' assent, which leg to mangle or which arm to tear off. To such an extent that—more from calculating the costs than from respect for the victims—the royal authorities in London relieved the beasts of their duties. But the hounds did not wish to abandon their post, not until a squadron of six royal soldiers of the same canine species were dispatched to drive them away. Then again, it seems that these dogs in Haiti could not have been more prepared for battle, given the way that Le Maître intervened—leaping, jaws wide open, at the neck of the first of Commandant Saurel's two mastiffs. Let's call him Mastiff One, and the second, Mastiff Two. Mastiff One stopped suddenly in his tracks, realized the tide was turning, and turned to face Ti Beau and Le Grand, who had just arrived on the scene on their own.

Mastiff One was a little portly and slow for its age and breed, most likely due to the bad influence of his master. After Le Maîre's assault, he took a fraction of a second too long to react and counterattack, which left him lingering pitifully on the ground in a defensive posture, snapping at the air. Pinned against a bench, wriggling and losing his sang-froid beneath the stately Le Maître, he could only fend of the inevitable. Meanwhile, Mastiff Two had already inflicted a nasty wound on Ti Beau and was dashing towards Le Grand, who was retreating while trying to ward off his opponent with his paws outstretched, his mouth agape, and his bark murderous. Mastiff Two's superior strength quickly overwhelmed Le Grand, who found himself pinned down, forgetting his primal instincts as a greyhound that allowed him to leap and strike from above. The battle might have ended there, were it not Le Maître's swift solidarity. Letting go of a tired Mastiff One, he came to his companions' aid, landing a violent headbutt to Mastiff Two's left flank, pushing him away. The two intrepid hounds, Mastiff Two and Le Maître, were suddenly facing each other. They paced in a circle, aware that all eyes were on them and that the outcome of their duel would decide the outcome of the general hostility.

*

From where Aïda stood on the verandah, she could feel the violence of the dogs' struggle wearing her down. From the very beginning of the chaos, since the moment the soldiers came to lead her out of her prison, Aïda had felt a strange unease, guided by something between her navel and her throat, a sadness she had known since she was a little girl. She discovered another shade of silence: one of solemnity rather than resignation. The soldiers came for her, and she followed them. She freed the dogs and walked along the path of isolation beside her mentor Dorilien, fully aware of the utter absurdity of the situation—as armed men came searching for a little girl, whose own destiny made no sense to her own self, under the pretext that she was a storyteller and might have participated in who-knows-what provincial rebellion.

She entered Balthazar's yard for the first time in her life, yet she could not tell the difference between the tribunal that had summoned her and the place that it had been before. Perhaps, she thought, Balthazar's house had always been like this. It seemed welcoming at first, but only to the children who quickly learnt how to suffer rather than how to read or count. From an early age, as she watched him preoccupied with his own image, smoking in silence with her mother and putting food on the table, Aïda had been aware of Balthazar's reputation for his rigid sense of honour and that he was feared by certain factions. Of late, especially since the sudden revelation of her inheritance, Aïda had begun to suspect that Balthazar had little to do with the image he so carefully projected. In the end, he might well have been a gentleman, or even a victim of the story, cast as the evildoer only to profit from the tranquillity that a clear conscience affords.

Aïda, however, the young renn chantrèl that she was, despite the limitless combinations and associations she could conjure from every nursery rhyme and story; despite the pain that she had begun to discern among the bits of wood representing peoples' feelings of remorse; despite her voice, which carried compassion for the rich as much as the poor, for objects as much as for animals, for embroiled monarchs as much as vanquished soldiers, for the mulattos as much as the whites—despite everything, Aïda had not yet realized the extent to which everyone is as much a prisoner as a victim, as guilty as they are innocent. Now was not the time to worry about all of this anthropodicy, the dogs had stopped pacing, and tensions were beginning to bubble over.

Mastiff Two's back paws were shaking, and he was ready to launch an attack when Aïda, from the back of the crowd, discovered her piercing scream. A scream that caused the schoolchildren to wince. A scream that shook the leaves and cast an aura of mystery around her. Aïda threw herself forward, arms open, into the echo of a powerful warning, leaving the verandah and rushing towards the disrupted, devastated tribunal. Just as she had been a few months earlier, when she recited her first story before everyone's eyes and ears, when she had become a renn chantrèl at her mother's wake, Aïda was once again alone before them all, caught up in a moment that marked a point of no return.

'That's enough!' She shouted. 'It's over. Stop this!'

The shock and surprise lasted hardly more than a few seconds, for Mastiff Two, seeing Aïda as the new adversary, abandoned Le

Maître, turned towards the young girl, and leapt with his mouth open, fangs bared. The dog latched onto the base of Aïda's neck, knocking her down and twisting her body from left to right. We will never know if this was the cause of general befuddlement, whether it was the roar of thunder that followed, or whether, of his own volition, Mastiff Two realized he had committed a grave mistake. The fact remains that he finally let go of Aïda and then attempted to flee, but his death was foretold by every one of his newfound enemies—animal and human alike—united against the perpetrator.

21

The rain had invited itself the night before, a kind of surprise visit, like a friend you no longer wait for because they never show up when expected. There was no bitterness towards the showers; instead, there was the tenacious malaise of an isolated people losing their way.

After the crazed hound had violently attacked Aïda, torn her neck with one single grasp, there was no debate over how to care for the wounded girl. The question first fell to Ludovic Possible, who quickly posed it to Brother Lélé, in whose house we now find the young girl lying on her back, eyes closed to this world and open to the next, as though in eternal rest.

There was no further discussion of the fate of the dog that had injured Aïda.

A certain calm had returned to the dark night. The wind and rain blew through the door panels, and Balthazar Possible was full of remorse, as though he had been caught and dragged by his shoulders. He went outside as soon as Francius informed him that, by his orders, the dog had been captured and tied up. Rifle in hand, he walked into the night, shaking, with the firm intention of executing the mastiff with a bullet between the eyes.

However, his intent did not take into account the humidity in the air, the hopeless mixture of gunpowder and rain, and, especially, the fact that, in all his life, despite an undeniably brutal past, Balthazar had never fired a rifle. Balthazar had only ever relied on his bare hands and his impressions of people, which Mastiff Two must have been unaware of—had the canine known, he would have been paralysed by his opponent's record. As soon as the dog saw Balthazar approach, he began to growl, trying to intimidate his opponent in his own right by baring his long canines, still sullied with little Aïda's blood. The dog's demeanour intensified Balthazar's wrath. He was too dour to feel the raindrops on his shoulders. Drawing a moment of wisdom from his grief, Balthazar leapt towards the beast, luring him with his left hand, and, just as Mastiff Two launched his attack, Balthazar planted the rifle's bayonet into the dog, once, twice, three times, crying his own tears of rage, ignoring the pain inflicted by the dog's last, failed bite. After the act of retribution, Balthazar returned to his seat on the verandah, then cleaned and dressed his wound. With no one around besides his soldiers, Balthazar was once again reminded of Aïda being taken away, forcing him to relive his hesitancy that had held him back from lending a hand or offering his soldiers' help in carrying the young girl to Brother Lélé's house. He watched as the small group of designated people left, the close-knit circle that notably excluded him: from Papa Possible to Bérénice Jean-Baptiste, all the way down to Timoléon, Jean-Zamor, Doréus, Dorilien and Altagrâce, everyone else following, like a funeral procession accompanying the wounded girl in Paloma Placide's and Mama Résia's arms. Each of them left with a piece of Balthazar, something that he was sure he had lost for ever, plucked from him like a bird's feathers, like the first act of his own dying. Amid the pain and remorse, he felt as though he had been relieved of his own sense of self, as though malice had left him once and for all—an unanticipated catharsis on a sombre afternoon in Boën.

*

A hand caressed Aïda's hair, but she was no longer with them. She was already on the other side, with Gracilia, on her childhood verandah. The mother and daughter conversing for an indefinite amount of time, particularly from the daughter's perspective, for she had been swindled out of the very notion of time in the hours after her injury.

Gracilia suddenly appeared before her, without forewarning:

'My child, how are you feeling?'

'Mama, stay with me. Don't leave me alone here in this violent world. You are the world to me. You are my life, my Cul-de-Sac. You're the world I've always known. Don't leave me here alone with these people.'

The night after Gracilia's burial, Aïda had seen her mother as she was now: serene, urging Aïda to persevere, to follow her own path, to resist being undone by dead-end stories, the ones that were inextricably bound to the earth, shared among the people living around her. Stories of cockfights, of fights between men and women, mulatto and Black; stories of nations and honour. The mother asked Aïda not to allow herself to succumb to the whims of adulthood, which require no preparation, repetition or practice of any kind. And finally, Gracilia added one last word:

'You are now a woman. You have been a renn chantrèl since my send-off. This is a way of life, a reason to persist. From now on, whenever you speak, whenever you recite stories, you will never be alone. You will have your words. You will have countless friends and innumerable foes, whom you will invent and shape in your own image. You will never be alone again.'

Despite her deceased mother's counsel, Aïda never ceased to feel solitude, like a pain pressing on her delicate neck. On this day, she did not want to leave Gracilia. She longed to remain with her on the verandah—the place where her mother used to brush her hair, where she so often cajoled her, guided her and, most importantly, told her stories. In the place where, together, they tackled humiliation head-on, wearing it like a silken veil placed between the two of them and the world. In the place where they witnessed the arrival of so many consolations, where they celebrated when tobacco was sold like hotcakes, where Balthazar stopped in to savour the news and a little piece of this or that, the place where the two of them were simply, quietly content.

*

The room in Brother Lélé's house was modest in size. In normal times, this was all that he needed, for despite his eternal bond with Mama Résia, Brother Lélé had always lived alone among the salves, carafes and scarves that adorned his walls and decorated his soul. It was not a question of space. His house and yard felt too small because along with Bérénice, Timoléon and Paloma; one will find the two brothers, Balthazar and Ludovic, standing front and centre around the bed that had been set up for Aïda.

They were standing elbow to elbow, silently, avoiding each other's gaze. We shall never know from whence Balthazar gathered the courage to appear at Brother Lélé's house tonight, immediately after skewering the mastiff, tending to his own wounds and reflecting on little Aïda. But if we were to enter the brothers' minds, perhaps we would find remnants of doubt, responsibility or even a touch of guilt for the problems they caused simply because of who they were: Balthazar, the bastard son of Pattieu Possible, a white Creole and property owner, and Josiane, known by the surname Mouliez, a free Black woman who was never emancipated; and Ludovic Possible, son of the same Pattieu Possible and of Adélicide Paul, a light-skinned mulatto woman of status, buried six-feet under a sentimental and sickly bruise. By being who they were, and by contorting themselves into uncompromising rivals, they might have caused all of this.

Perhaps we would find in their minds, too, as in that of little Aïda lying before them, the presence of a woman, Gracilia France Placide, with whom they were both acquainted, and perhaps even loved in their own strange ways. The two brothers were right there, and yet they knew no prayer, no ritual capable of bringing back the young storyteller so violently attacked by a dog.

Besides these two gentlemen, the scent of basil applied to Aïda's wound filled much of the room. It mingled with the smell of the earth, made fresh outside by the pouring rain. No one seemed concerned about the potential damage, even if they would have to relive a diluvian drama. Apart from the fixer men and rainmakers, whose fraudulence was constant and widely acknowledged, there was no way to combat the rain falling from the sky. There were, however, appropriate ways of caring for the gravely wounded, especially those who had been violently attacked by dogs, and lost consciousness for more than ten hours. In such therapeutic matters, Mama Résia's plants and Brother Lélé's botanical resources worked well together. Not that plants were always friendly with one another, or particularly beneficial to humans—it was just that Mama Résia and Brother Lélé knew how to tame them, solicit their assistance and negotiate the best results.

Brother Lélé rubbed aloe vera, known as *lalwa*, on Aïda's face and under her arms, reciting his four words as he lit the candles on his altar, taking the opportunity, he said, to initiate the young woman into seeing through from the other side. More simply, Mama Résia sponged the gaping wound, applied basil and a few essential oils and placed almond leaves on the soles of the girl's feet. Everyone waited in silence, stunned by collective fear.

*

Paloma's hand slid through Aïda's hair once more—a simple gesture that opened the great, universal reservoir of tenderness.

On the verandah where Gracilia spoke to her daughter, the same scent of basil arose with something else—a whiff of cold tobacco.

'Now, open your eyes!' Gracilia said to her daughter.

She knew that, on the other side of the water, Pépé the Tempest was waiting for her chance to be a mother once more.

'Now, open your eyes, Aïda.' whispered Paloma, her lips trembling as she swallowed her tears. Aïda, renn chantrèl of your country, you still have words to carry, mysteries to unravel.'

'My eyes are wide open, and I see you,' Aïda replied.

Aïda closed her eyes to this world only to open them to the other, or perhaps she had closed them in the other world only to open them to this one, a world that awaited her words, her silences and her stories of repair and restitution.

Translator's Afterword

> Aïda, far from being mute, searched for her words deep in the back of her throat, sometimes further still, into her soul—where her words found their precision and strength.

Duels is a novel about the power of storytelling. These stories are passed down from generation to generation, carried from the coast of Africa to the shores of Haiti, sung at the edge of a swollen river, whispered at a child's bedside, recited in a jail cell and wailed at a wake. In every one of these instances, words become imbued with the power to transform, translate and alleviate the anxieties that weigh on the storyteller and their audience. Stories offer deliverance from the inhospitality of the real through the gentle embrace of the imaginary, transporting listeners, readers and storytellers to worlds where anything is possible so long as it can be imagined.

Translating *Duels* has entailed a process of recasting the stories, carrying them from one idiom to another and resetting them to a new rhythm that recalls the flow of the original while allowing for the novelty and invention of the language of translation. In a way, my path as a translator was not unlike the one Aïda takes in the novel, where writing the novel anew involved looking both within and without to find words that could tell the story with precision and strength. The years I have spent reading and studying Haitian language and literature guided me in handling the four languages Néhémy Dahomey employs in *Duels*—French, Haitian Creole, English and Spanish—a narrative trait that he shares with other Haitian writers such as Jacques Stephen Alexis, Jan J. Dominique, Edwidge Danticat and others. By allowing these languages to mingle and coexist in the English translation, I sought to preserve the island-wide bonds between Haiti and the Dominican Republic, bonds that are forged and frayed as the story unfolds. Just as Dahomey does in the original, I hope my choice to retain expressions of intimate address like *commère* and *compère,* and terms like *renn chantrèl* or *lodyanseur* in either French or Haitian Creole will imbue the translation with an indelible sense of place.

The world of literary allusions in *Duels* extends beyond the choice of language, as Dahomey embeds references to Haitian literature, both written and oral, throughout the novel. Some of these are more explicit than others. For example, when Paloma Placide learns of Gracilia's passing, she is overcome with emotion in *L'espace d'un cillement*, echoing the title of the last novel Jacques Stephen Alexis published before he was murdered by François Duvalier's secret police, the Tonton Mahout. To retain this reference, I drew on the phrasing of Carol F. Coates and Edwidge Danticat's English translation of Alexis's novel, *In the Flicker of an Eyelid*, hoping readers will follow the same trail of breadcrumbs Dahomey leaves in the French original. Another textual allusion in the Haitian cultural and literary imaginary is the phrase 'personal property', which I have translated into English and paired with the words in French *biens meubles* in this volume. This line is drawn from Article 44 of the 1685 Code Noir (Black Code), issued by King Louis XIV of France to assert control over its Caribbean colonies and the captive Africans forced to cultivate sugar, coffee, indigo and other cash crops. The Code Noir, and specifically Article 44, declared that enslaved people in France's Caribbean colonies were to be considered property—bought, sold and traded like furniture or other moveable goods. Although the Code Noir was no longer in force during the period in which *Duels* is set—Haitian independence in 1804 and the abolition of slavery had overthrown the French rule—traces of the colonial era remain deeply embedded in the minds and bodies of the characters. By preserving and echoing 'personal property, *biens meubles*' in translation, I wish to suggest, as Dahomey does in the original, that the history of slavery and its violent legacy remain very much alive in its wake.

Another profound cultural and literary allusion in *Duels* is the Haitian oral storytelling tradition in known as *lodyans* (audience), led by a male *lodyanseur,* a female *lodyanseuse.* There are many *lodyanseurs* in *Duels,* but the novel is propelled by the ongoing verbal jousting between the young Aïda and Big-Bellied Dorilien. A hallmark of the lodyans genre is the call-and-response structure, which demands both the attention and the participation of the audience to animate the performance. In translating one of these calls, I intentionally spliced another allusion to Haitian literature. In the French original, Dahomey employs the French spelling of the lodyanseur's call 'Cric?' and 'Crac!' for the audience's response. In my translation, I chose the Haitian Creole spelling 'Krik? Krak!' The difference may seem negligible or simply a matter of preference, but adopting the Haitian Creole orthography embeds a deliberate reference to Edwidge Danticat's debut collection of short stories of the same name, a homage to other works of Haitian literature available in English. I describe this as splicing because, had I chosen to retain Dahomey's spelling, it too would have echoed the title of another work of Haitian literature—Georges Sylvain's 1901 collection, *Cric? Crac!: Fables de La Fontaine racontées par un montagnard haïtien* (Cric? Crac!: La Fontaine's Fables as Told by a Haitian Man of the Hills). While these works, like *Duels*, stand on their own and create their own fabulous realms of fiction, they nonetheless echo one another and belong to the vast repertoire of Haitian written and oral narratives. As a translator, I feel it is my role to make sure that these references, among many others, are preserved as playfully as the author intended so that readers may look to the literature of the past for ways to narrate the future.

Acknowledgements

*

FROM THE AUTHOR

Many thanks to:

The Residence de Pure Fiction, Occitanie Livre and especially to Isabel Desesquelles;

The Festival of Books in Mouans-Sartoux and the writer's residency;

The writing workshop in the city of Angers and the Toussaint Médiathèque;

The CROUS Lorraine residency in Nancy, especially to Marie-Madeleine Rigopoulos.

The author recognizes the support of the Centre National du Livre (CNL) of France while writing this novel.

*

FROM THE TRANSLATOR

All translators deserve compassionate editors, ample resources and a community of support. I am fortunate to have all of these in my life. I began this translation in a small town in Ohio and completed it in Saint Louis, Missouri, on the banks of an unbendable river, in the place we now call home. I could not have completed this translation without the tireless support of my friends and family, Jocelyn Sutton Franklin, Annette Joseph-Gabriel, Corine Labridy, Siobhan Meï, Jennifer Boum Make, Laëtitia Saint-Loubert, Erika V. Serrato, Lucy Swanson, Vanessa K. Valdés, Charly Verstraet and, especially, Katherine McKenna, who guided me through the meanderings of this journey.

I am grateful to have worked with the editorial team at Seagull Books. Thank you, as always, for your patience.

I also want to express my gratitude to Néhémy Dahomey for entrusting me with his words. We began working together on another novel years ago, and little did we know that this would be the first translation to appear in English.

Last, and certainly not least, a measure of gratitude is due to Natália Affonso for lending the kindest ear, providing the most constructive feedback, and carefully doulaing this translation into being during a very tender moment in my life. *Mèsi konmè mwen, mèsi anpil anpil.*